The People's President

The People's President

IN THE NATION'S SERVICE

JOHN C. BEDNAR

Archway Publishing books may be ordered through booksellers or by contacting:

Archway Publishing
1663 Liberty Drive
Bloomington, IN 47403
www.archwaypublishing.com
1 (888) 242-5904

Because of the dynamic nature of the Internet, any web addresses or links contained in this book may have changed since publication and may no longer be valid. The views expressed in this work are solely those of the author and do not necessarily reflect the views of the publisher, and the publisher hereby disclaims any responsibility for them.

Any people depicted in stock imagery provided by Thinkstock are models, and such images are being used for illustrative purposes only. Certain stock imagery © Thinkstock.

ISBN: 978-1-4808-3901-4 (sc)
ISBN: 978-1-4808-3902-1 (e)

Library of Congress Control Number: 2016917448

Print information available on the last page.

Archway Publishing rev. date: 10/28/2016

1

In the dark halls and stately shadows
Of greatness superimposed on knowledge,
Do we ever stop to find the trace
Of meaning forced into a corner?
In the driving, vicious disturbance
Of perpetuating greatness,
Do we search to defend the
Poet's right to speak?
In passing through the hallowed
Ivy walls of wisdom incarnate,
Do we stand to say that we
Are here to find and seek?
While the blazing light of our
Glorious name protrudes for us,
Do we lift our minds
And stand in awe of truth?
No.

George Franklin turned the piece of yellowed paper in his hands and smiled at the sentiment of his aging mother, who had sent him the poem. It was written on loose-leaf, the kind used by college students, and he couldn't remember when he had received it. Probably during his sophomore year at Princeton, while he was leading a one-man battle against snobbery and the eating clubs. Or maybe later.

He leaned back in his office chair, propped his feet up, and reread the lines slowly. For some reason, the original context failed to reappear, and he saw instead the world around him—a country he had been taught to love ruining itself by refusing the humility of truth. The wars, the bloody upheavals, senseless killing—American power gone wrong. Wasn't it strange how all the "truth" and "meaning" were so easily pushed off into a corner?

George was now a distinguished professor of political science at his alma mater, Princeton University. He had taught there for a number of years. A lot of the rebellion was in the past, and he had worked hard to establish himself as a respected scholar and teacher. Like many of his colleagues, he marched pretty much to the beat of his own drum, but that was part of the Princeton tradition, individual thinking. All knew that he would speak his own mind while respecting and defending their right to do the same thing. All in all, he was well liked not only on campus but also throughout the community of political researchers in the United States and abroad.

For a good while, he sat reading the poem and mulling over the last word. *No, no, no.* Nobody appeared to be willing to change the marasmus of silly game playing—in business, education, the military, or elsewhere. Sure, there were plenty of groups out there deluding themselves into thinking they were accomplishing something. All the political activists and spin-city specialists were simply turning the world upside down. They didn't realize that they were doing little more than having a nice day. And in his mind, the political scene was a genuine catastrophe.

As he continued to ponder, an old feeling welled up inside like the urge to urinate. He knew it well. His youthful idealism and outspokenness had been the cause of more than one halt in promotion through the years. It was one of those gushers of inexplicable forces that grabs a human being and drags him into the abyss. For some, it was gambling; others, women; and for most, money. For George Franklin, it was fighting the odds—refusing to buckle to the will of the crowd. How many times had he wanted to scream in some poor salesperson's face, "No, I won't have a nice day. I'll have a challenging, fruitful, and *hard* day!" He never said it, but his closest friends knew that was the way he reacted. George was a leader and a fighter.

The old feeling grew stronger and stronger. "I'm more mature now," he thought out loud. "I have a solid marriage, and I should be more realistic." But it was no use. The catalyst of years of fighting for the principle burning in his mind, rekindled by the poem, was too strong. It was an unavoidable trigger mechanism. When he reached that point, George Franklin went into action mode. His socially more-reserved colleagues had seen it in faculty meetings and were used to it. Because of his widespread popularity and excellent teaching, nobody wanted to get rid of him. But they would leave the door ajar just in case he slipped up and went too far. Franklin was not dangerous in their minds, but he might well screw up their day to the point that they would never have a nice one again.

George's eyes lit upon the thin Princeton telephone book gathering dust on his windowsill. He took off the fat Trenton directory on top of it and began searching under A until he came to "Associated Press, 50 West State Street, (609) 392-3622." His right hand jotted down the number on an old envelope while he pulled out his cell phone and flipped it open to make a call.

"Good morning, Associated Press."

"Good morning. This is Professor Franklin at Princeton. I have an announcement to make to the press. Could you connect me with the right person?" He was calm, sure of himself, and made no effort to resist the feeling.

"One moment," said the receptionist, followed by a slight pause.

"Rogers here."

"Mr. Rogers, this is Professor Franklin at Princeton University."

"Yes?"

"I have an announcement to make to the press, and I've been put through to you as the person who should take it."

"Subject?"

"What do you mean?"

"Education, society, sports, discovery, politics—you know."

"Politics. I'm running for the presidency of the United States."

"What?"

"That's right. And I want you to put this down verbatim. Are you listening?"

"Uh … yeah."

"Professor George B. Franklin, presently a full professor in the Political Science Department of Princeton University, is an official candidate for the presidency of the United States. He is an Independent, adhering to no political party, and will apply two basic principles to his entire campaign. The first is that he will not spend a dime of his own money to become elected. The second is that he will not accept a penny from anyone else in the form of contributions. Did you get that?" George had spoken very slowly.

"Yeah … but I don't believe it. What are you, some kind of nut? The primaries are almost over and done with."

"Just put it on the wire, Mr. Rogers. If you want verification, send one of your reporters to see me. Otherwise, you'll have a letter on official university stationery tomorrow. I'm very serious."

George hung up. The surge of conviction running through his veins was like adrenaline to the long-distance runner. He was himself, convinced he was right, and lopping off about the biggest chunk of odds fighting in his life. It was great. He was through with sitting behind his desk and criticizing and was now on his way to being the next president of the United States.

It was an election year, mid-April, and the sun was shining in New Jersey.

II.

Larry Stanton had been hounded all morning by telephone calls from more than fifteen major cities. They were all asking the same embarrassing questions and getting the same noncommittal answers. Why hadn't Milton Wagner disclosed his Florida land deals to the public *before* the New York primary? How could his failure to pay income taxes on all that dough have gone unexplained until now? How could a crook like that get so far? How the hell did he expect to get his candidate elected president of the United States now? And that wasn't all; e-mail messages were clogging his in-box asking for the immediate refund of campaign contributions in light of such a blatantly ridiculous scandal. His cell phone went straight to voice mail. To put it mildly, he was exasperated.

Larry scratched his head and looked at the incoherent scribbling in front of him. It was hard for him to face the truth of what was happening. You don't just give up faith and trust and loyalty over a lukewarm cup of coffee and a half-eaten doughnut. Hell, he wouldn't have dreamed in a million years that Milt Wagner was such a monumental con man. He had really believed in the guy. He had even thought of him as a kind of savior, one who could lead, make a difference.

"Mr. Stanton? Chicago on line two." Miss Stewart broke his train of thought.

"Hello? Stanton? What in the name of merry hell is going on out there? Do you flatheads think the Democratic Party will ever win another election?" It was Harry Logan, probably the most influential Democrat in the Midwest.

"Take it easy, Harry. Slow down—"

"Slow down? Hell! I'll do more than that. I'll stop! This is the stupidest slipup I've ever seen. You guys win all those primaries and then get caught on *income taxes?*"

It went on and on, just like the others. No, he didn't know what they were going to do. That was up to Wagner. A statement would be forthcoming. Be patient.

The pressure was too much. Larry slammed his fist on the desk, like a karate chop, and almost broke it in two. The paperweight went flying, and his glasses fell on the floor. He reached down to pluck them up hurriedly and put them back on his nose, frustrated.

As he looked up at a startled Miss Stewart standing at the door, he said, "Mary, would you tell the senator I'd like to see him?"

"He's in conference with Judge Wilson, Mr. Stanton. Could you wait?" She had that mechanical look of oblivion on her face, although the noise obviously didn't go along with her idea of a normal workday.

"No. But that doesn't make any difference." Larry, surprising himself, adjusted his glasses, looked deep into her expressionless eyes, and said, "Just tell him to go to hell!"

And with that, he strolled out of the office, hardly believing what he had just done.

Larry Stanton was the most capable and professional campaign manager in the United States. He knew more about the computerized technology of modern politics than anyone. It was Stanton who had perfected a system of instant communication with his entire organization. His efficient use of propaganda was respected all over Washington. Larry Stanton, with his red moustache and his New York accent and his youthful good looks (in spite of his age), had engineered a miraculous revival of Democratic unity—or so he thought. And here he was, walking off the job.

He recoiled at the surface stupidity of it all, but it was frighteningly true. The challenge of putting Milton Wagner, US senator, in the White House had suddenly vanished. With a trite, vulgar phrase, he had changed the course of his life. Even Mary Stewart (yes, her real name) was taken aback. She probably had composed herself by now, though, and would be telling the senator that "Larry was feeling the pressure." Larry fed on pressure, but not that kind. You had to be crazy to continue fighting for a 100 percent loser. He was getting out now and washing his hands of Milt for good. Larry was also in the abyss.

Larry grumbled to himself all the way home. He was sick and tired of the whole crowd. Wagner had played everyone for a fool and gotten away with it. "Think they'd learn," he mumbled, his ego hurting a lot more than he was willing to admit. He entered his Fifth Avenue Manhattan condo and, like an automaton, shut off the alarm and video surveillance system, and then he took five paces to the right. Reaching down, he switched on the stereo that connected to a surround sound system set on a classical music station, *his* oblivion. Larry made a sudden decision to walk over to his bar area and chose a cold imported beer out of his wine chiller. "Beer—at least *that's* still trustworthy," he said and slouched in a chair. He then questioned his own comment when his gaze caught a fully unopened can of Billy Beer on his shelf, next to a picture of Jimmy Carter, bearing a date of October 1980. He looked at his beer, shook his head left and right, took another sip, and smirked at the irony the universe was bequeathing him on this day.

The home was quite opulent. Upon entering, one noticed Italian marble floor tiles, and on the foyer walls hung original French impressionist paintings from the Nabi period, depicting flat colors and Japanese-inspired composition. An oil painting by Pierre Bonnard of a well-dressed aristocratic man with hat in hand bowing to another lesser-dressed man was strategically placed directly ahead at eye level upon entering, flanked on the left wall by a rustic oil painting of a group of laborers on a farm by Edward Vuillard. On the right wall, just before the entry into the living room, hung a painting exuding bright-yellow hues, in pointillistic style, by George Seurat, depicting a group of upper-class men engaged in discussion as they enjoyed beverages.

The decor was further enhanced by the limestone imported from Paris, and the attention to detail in the construction of the walls and crown molding was a perfect replica of the interior of a small chateau built in 1724. Each piece of antique furniture was carefully selected and complemented by enhancements, old lamps, antique corkscrews, and sculptures. Federal end tables held historical books, and outside of the kitchen facing an unlit large LED television screen was an arrow back Windsor chair built in 1825. One of only a handful of existing sculptures by Edgar Degas beckoned you to enter the living room. There was no dust, as a housekeeper visited every other day. Larry took off his shoes and placed them neatly in a space for them by the leather couch.

"You have just heard the Horowitz recording of Beethoven's

Waldstein Sonata, an old LP in a new digital rework but recognized by many critics as the finest recording of this piece in existence. Now for the news." The commentator capsulized the Wagner explosion with short, crisp sentences. Then he added, "An unusual event, aside from the Democratic fiasco, has occurred on the political scene. Apparently, an obscure, unknown college professor has decided to enter the presidential race late in the game. His name is Dr. George B. Franklin, and he is a distinguished professor of political science at Princeton University in New Jersey. He belongs to no political party, declaring himself an Independent. According to Professor Franklin, he will not accept any money from others for his campaign, nor will he spend a dime of his own funds. Political pressures seem to be creeping into the hallowed walls of academia and stirring up the dust of the classroom. Our best wishes to Dr. Franklin, naive as his approach may be."

The pupils in Larry Stanton's eyes were the size of quarters.

III.

James Singleton, far from the crisis of scandal in the enemy camp, beamed as he put down the blue telephone in his luxurious office. The office was composed of dark wood, floor to ceiling, with built-in shelves and alcoves filled with books and self-serving photos with well-known figures. He sat in a large, high-back, oxblood leather chair with burled edges. The guest chairs across his desk were wide, more rigid, and with leather cushions that had craquelure and scrapes from years of use. Atop the pecan hardwood floor lay a Hamadan Persian rug, with bright cobalt and maroon colors, worn in the center from foot traffic. The smell of Cuban cigar odor permeated the furniture and was partially overpowered by Singleton's musk cologne, upon which he depended to conceal the scent of alcohol emanating from his lips. He had just learned of Wagner's debacle, one that he himself had carefully prepared, covering his tracks like an Indian. No one knew or could even find out that he had pushed Wagner into the fire. It was too well prepared and dated back too many years.

He was ecstatic. Politics—dirty, gutsy politics—were his thing. And the news of his successful *coup* made him jump up and down inside. He even did a little jig, like Hitler in his alpine retreat.

"Jack," as his closest acquaintances referred to him, was the work-horse of traditional American politics. Little could be said for his private life. Nobody knew much about it. But everyone on Capitol Hill knew him. As a young man, he had blossomed in some faraway congressional district and ever since had belonged to Washington's ken. When the Republican Party, suffering from its image as a bunch of liars, cheats, and money-grubbers, mustered enough enthusiasm to push him for the presidency, Jack suddenly came alive, as though he had been waiting for the opportunity to show that he was the man for the job. Despite his age, he garnered enough support to put him in the number-one position. There certainly was no indication on the surface that anyone suspected his carefully laid-out plan. The smile on his face resembled that of a hungry wolf, about to finish its prey. Wagner had been considerably more careless than he had anticipated, not checking into his finances as far as he should have. Now that he was completely screwed, the funny thing was that Wagner would believe it was his own error! From this point on, the race was won, and Singleton could enjoy a little pure contentment.

"Jack?" A knock at the door to his plush suite of rooms announced the arrival of Howard Carlyle. Howard was his campaign manager, in name only. Jack did all the real work and didn't even let Howard in on what he was doing most of the time.

"Did you hear?"

"Yeah."

"Who from?"

"Some more-or-less spies that I know."

"It's breaking on the news. You must be happy as hell."

"You bet I am." Jack was ebullient, more so than he could let on to Carlyle. He knew that his own genius had been responsible for ev-erything but could only show a tenth of his zeal to the unsuspecting confidant. Some sharp investigative reporters had uncovered the trash, just at the right moment, and no one knew they were on Singleton's payroll, not even themselves. This was super politics, the most refined in the business, a moment of supreme bliss to be appreciated.

"Howard, I think we're in!" He clapped poor little Carlyle on the shoulder like a football player and offered him a cigar. "Pollute my office. I'll join you!"

The two puffed merrily on the first couple of drags, letting the smoke curl up toward the ceiling and diffuse itself throughout the spacious room. Carlyle, he knew, was on another track. He already saw himself as secretary of something, gallivanting around the country (or the world) and giving smug talks on college campuses.

Howard Carlyle—distinguished equivalent to Larry Stanton—was an altogether different man. The Republicans had been forced to choose an impeccable figurehead after all the dirt they had been through. Carlyle filled the bill. A square-jawed poster boy for the Boy Scouts. The poor fellow knew nothing about running a political campaign—or anything else, for that matter—but he was popular with the moneymen and appealed to the Christian Coalition crowd. That meant cash on the line and confidence not to be destroyed. Singleton handled the secret payments himself with a system of laundering so perfect it would never fail. Carlyle buttered the surface like a piece of bread and everybody loved him.

Howard (only his wife occasionally called him "Howie") was a smooth talker and a basically insouciant lover of wealth. This may have explained his success. He inspired the rich with a feeling they were important and appreciated, and his manner was that of an equal. The Carlyle fortune could vie with any respectable lump of cash in the country, and "Howie" was an only child. Some of the more influential families of American power even felt a tinge of jealousy because the concentration of wealth seemed to increase as the Carlyle's diminished in number. All of this because "Howie" had gone one step beyond his prolific ancestors and failed to reproduce a single offspring. In today's world, that meant no child-oriented expenses—and no worries. The lucky bastard. He was clearly an example of Republican ideals. He even allayed, somewhat, the masses' fears concerning political corruption, being basically blind to it himself. He had accepted the job of campaign manager for Jack Singleton because that fit into his idea of service to the nation. He was too naive to see that Jack was pulling the strings backstage and sufficiently bourgeois enough not to care, even if he found out.

The arrangement was usually the other way around, but circumstances had made the money collector more important, superficially, than the candidate himself.

"Let's catch the news," bubbled Singleton, pulling a bottle of Dom Perignon from his private office reserve.

They ate up every word, as Wolf Blitzer tried to maintain his calm reporter's voice. Excitement was unknown to the TV veteran, but it was there, behind the words. As the two cronies listened, the analysis of the newscaster appeared sensational. "The Democratic Party will have to swallow hard before it digests this one. Politics in America have taken a strange twist. Rapid justice will undoubtedly be demanded by the public at large, and the Democratic Party will be scratching its head trying to come up with a viable candidate at this late date."

Unbelievable, fantastic. They would float through November like they were floating now and bury those liberal so-and-so's along the way.

Jack and Howard were about to turn off the set, dripping the last bit of champagne into their crystal coupes, when they heard Blitzer add his last bit of humor at the end of the broadcast.

"As a humorous note to today's political upheavals, we have just learned that Dr. George B. Franklin—professor of political science, of all things—at Princeton University has entered the race for the White House. Shunning both major parties and completely unknown in the dog-eat-dog arena, Professor Franklin says that he will not spend one dime of his own money for his campaign, nor will he accept a penny from anyone else. According to our calculations, that gives him just nine cents to become president of the United States."

Singleton burped and the two clinked their glasses in a sign of victory, ignoring what they had just heard.

IV.

Charlie Gibson, retired from being a news anchor and recently retired from being on the board of trustees at Princeton, was delighted with Wolf Blitzer's humor, and equally curious—so much so that he was already on the phone, frantically trying to get hold of the professor on his campus who had managed to attract enough attention to get his name on national television. The name was only vaguely familiar to him.

"Telephone Directory"—he clicked on the bookmark on his computer to find out the guy's number and address. He assumed, naturally, that the man was part of the heterogeneous set they all were familiar with at Princeton. This story had to be good enough for a few laughs, and Charlie wanted to both beat all his colleagues to the punch and also try to save face for Princeton, if necessary. He used to be in charge of newscasting—or, at least, he seemed to show the most energy in that domain—but he stood out from his group. More often than not, he was the loner who went out and found the unusual bit of oomph to brighten up the story. An extremely conscientious reporter, nevertheless, he let his friends lay out the common, everyday news and was always looking for big bait. His old station did a pretty good job, he thought, of saying things the right way, but it lacked sensational news, the kind today's viewers wanted every time they zapped on their TV sets.

Charlie grabbed his school directory, but it did not list the home number. He called a friend, and bingo! George B. Franklin in Princeton proper on Hillside Road.

Charlie's fingers, fingers that had typed millions of words, flew over greasy numbers on his cell phone. Busy. Darn it! Somebody must have scooped him. He wondered why the original news release on the AP wire hadn't given more information. How could something like that be out for six hours without a reference check? Why hadn't someone at Princeton told him about it? He pressed the redial button.

"Hello?" a calm voice answered.

"Professor Franklin?"

"Yes."

"This is Charlie Gibson calling. I'd like to know a little more about your declaration to the press today. Do you mind?"

"Not at all. You must have just watched Wolf Blitzer. He and I attended a conference together on international relations many years ago. Knowing Wolf, though, I'm not surprised at his humor. What can I do for you?" Charlie thought he heard a little irony or maybe some personal humor behind the voice.

"Well, I'd like to interview you, and I thought maybe I could set it up for this evening." Charlie was pressing, sure that someone else was first. "Could you come into the city?"

"I'm flattered by your interest, but I seem to sense a little—how should I say this—sensation-hunting in your voice. The press release was perfectly clear, and I fully intend to live up to it. On top of that, I will not play anyone's game of ridicule, nor will I titillate the viewers on any station's programs. If you have intelligent questions to ask, I'll be very glad to answer them. Otherwise, please don't call again."

"Well … I—"

"I don't mean to sound impolite, Charlie, but I think you should understand that I'm deadly serious. Tell you what, if you are curious enough to see for yourself who I am, why don't you come out to the house around eight? We'll be expecting you."

The man really did sound serious.

His voice was not haughty, tricky, or sly—which is what Gibson had half-expected—it glistened with simple assurance. How could this man possibly believe that a mobile team would jump in a van and go to him, when he had just received a better invitation for publicity than most cranks ever got in a lifetime? Charlie wasn't sure and hesitated for a few seconds.

"It's just that in a studio—" Charlie had access to one.

"Charlie, I'll leave it up to you. Right now, you probably think that this is a stunt of some kind. And I don't blame you. Anyone would think that after listening to Wolf's little commentary. You'll just have to choose whether or not you want to exercise the right I've just given you to satisfy your curiosity. Incidentally, Susan has taken a lot of calls like this all day long."

"We'll be there."

What was going on? Did this unknown clown know more about what he was doing than Gibson thought? A *political science professor* for president? Charlie thought that *he* had been an instigator of sensational and interesting stories on public television, but this guy seemed to be a step ahead of him. Maybe he had been a journalist or something unique in his past.

Charlie hung up the phone and chuckled. If this were a wild goose chase, it was the funniest one he had seen in a long time. Acting fast, he called an old friend with a camera crew (who were on call, like fighter pilots in a defense squadron) and literally ran down the hall. In less than three minutes, they would be on the road. And he needed those minutes to start a check.

"Hello? Urban? This is Charlie Gibson. Listen, I'm on my way down the turnpike to interview your Professor Franklin, who has just made a crazy announcement that he is a candidate for the presidency. Would you please fill me in on what kind of an animal this guy is?"

"I half expected you to call. I saw Wolf Blitzer's broadcast. How much time do you have?"

"We're loading the van right now. It's about an hour's drive."

"Dynamic, outspoken, popular as hell with the students, knowledgeable in more fields than you can count. One of his books is required reading for freshmen across the country. Trouble is, he doesn't fit into any mold—oh, I know, universities aren't supposed to have molds, but they do. Refuses to play the game. Hell, I don't know; you may like him. As you know, we have a lot of professors like that at Princeton." Urban went on and on as they rolled down Highway 1.

Finally, Charlie said, "Thanks, Urb, you're a big help."

Princeton was a booming university town, and finding Hillside Road was a piece of cake with Charlie's state-of-the-art GPS. Situated in a shaded lane that had been there for years, it wound around forever. Old, two-story houses that were solid middle class flew past the windows.

Charlie pondered over the meaning of what he was doing. He was so used to the normal set of pieces for the world's jigsaw puzzle. This one didn't seem to fit. He knew as an experienced newsman that you didn't get mentioned on national TV without creating a story. In the worst of circumstances, this one would be good for at least two days. And after all, with the number of murders and regular horrors going on, this seemed like a pleasant interlude to your run-of-the-mill stuff the news usually broadcast. As they pulled up in front of the house, Charlie promised his crew a nice dinner if they had come all that way for nothing.

V.

A six-foot, well-built, sincere-looking man in his late fifties answered the door and grasped Charlie's hand with a firm grip. His hair was heavily overcast with gray and silver, blue eyes; he couldn't be more *normal*. He actually looked more like a businessman than a professor. Charlie had half expected to find a disheveled long-hair (or maybe a baldy), but here was a man still in his tie and long-sleeved, white shirt, short haircut, clean-shaven. Respect and genuine hospitality seemed to reign as he and his crew came in—perhaps a little more formality than they were used to in the big city, but straightforward and kind.

They arranged two armchairs in the living room and began setting up the cameras and lighting equipment. The small house was modest and clean, a typical middle-class home. A back porch made of redwood could be seen from the living room.

"Before we get started, Charlie, would you like some coffee? We generally have some after dinner."

"Thanks anyway, Professor, but we'll be pressed for time." He would have loved a cup, all the more because he sensed it would be delicious, maybe French, but he thought it was better to refuse.

This feeling soon changed, however. Charlie Gibson, for all his apprehensions, began to feel at home. This man was smart but simple, about as genuine as they came. And Charlie's guard began to fall.

The crew finished in short order and they sat down for the interview, microphones attached and makeup artist finishing with some light brushing.

Charlie explained that he would not sensationalize and planned to ask simple questions, but the professor gave him a hard look and warned, "Don't be surprised if I ask you a few." The cameras began to roll.

"This is Charlie Gibson, coming out of retirement. Tonight, we are visiting with Dr. George B. Franklin, professor of political science at Princeton University. As many of you may already know, Professor Franklin has declared that he is a candidate for the office of president of the United States. He has made his announcement very late in this election year and is totally unknown in politics.

"The most unique aspect of his campaign is that Dr. Franklin plans to operate from start to finish with a budget of zero. He refuses to spend any of his own money and won't accept any contributions. On the face of it, this simply sounds preposterous to anyone who has ever run for public office. Dr. Franklin, with these restrictions, how can you wage any kind of a campaign?"

Gibson knew from the outset that his public would be much more interested in this question of money than in the man. The American public, after all, could always be counted on to think in terms of money. Although a few exceptions had occasionally popped up.

"With people like you, Charlie. You've shown enough interest to come all the way out to my home for an interview, mainly out of curiosity, but the fact is that you have done it. There is no reason that the organs of public information, like television, radio, newspapers, and the Internet, with all its social media, should fail to act as valid lines of communication between political candidates and the public—at no cost to the candidate. That is, after all, your primary function. But what I'd like to know, Charlie, is how seriously you accept that responsibility."

Bam! The tables were all of a sudden turned and the interviewer was being interviewed, put on the spot in front of his own audience.

"Are you saying, Professor Franklin, that the news media and social media will be your means of communication with the American people?" Charlie was slowly beginning to feel the thrill of a discovery. They had all been pushing people around for years, molding the news to fit their own limited conceptions of what they were doing. Vaguely, somewhere off in the distance, the guidelines were coming from their producers. And here was someone telling them that they had a communication responsibility that didn't have anything to do with how much money they were generating through the ratings.

"Why don't you answer my question first and then I'll answer yours?" The guy definitely was not playing around.

"I agree with you, Professor, and try to live up to that ideal every day."

"Don't call me 'Professor.' Mr. Franklin is fine."

Hell, he *was* leading the interview!

"Essentially, Charlie, I am depending on the same sense of responsibility that makes our democracy work and our nation potentially very great indeed. You and the other members of the media will report what you think should be reported. Some of you will accept bribes for what you say, bribes or threats from above. Others will be influenced in other ways. And the American people, in turn, will either respond positively to what you say or reject it. In most cases, they will accept, because you have learned how to appeal to their dollar-oriented surface. In short, Charlie, you are selling the news and the American people are consuming it, the same way they consume toothpaste. But what all of you seem to have forgotten is that all of those people, docile as they may appear to you, have the final say in things. And money is not necessarily the prime mover. Nor should it be. That's what my campaign is all about."

"In effect, Mr. Franklin, your campaign could end with this interview." Gibson had to know who else was coming over the next day.

"Doubtful, Charlie, very doubtful. You can cover up the truth for long periods of time, but it has a way of shining through in the end. The people who vote for me will understand that they are really voting for themselves—and accepting a great deal of personal responsibility when they do it."

"Let's talk about your reasons for wanting to be president. What makes a political science professor, unknown in politics and the public eye, declare his candidacy?" Charlie Gibson began to feel that he already knew the answer.

"I think the American people need to have a candidate *elected* by them and not *sold* to them. In order to demonstrate the fallacy of what I would call commercial politics, I have declared that money will simply not be a part of my campaign. In addition, I humbly think that I can bring some new thoughts to bear on American life. All of my endeavors will be in that direction. Oh, I know a lot of people have a stereotyped image of the college professor who thinks he knows it all, but I don't go for that pseudo-intellectual image. We have to start doing something constructive about the *quality* of our lives. And I think a far greater number of citizens in this country are ready to do that than anyone imagines."

This reply caught Charlie Gibson smiling—stupidly. As he realized that his face was that of a skeptic, he was not proud of himself. But he knew that his viewers would feel the same way. Or would they? This guy had something on the ball that demanded attention. His face changed.

"What are the major lines of your campaign, Mr. Franklin?" Charlie still wanted to call him "Professor."

"They are obviously ideal in nature, Mr. Gibson, yet realistic in purpose. One of my main concerns is in the field of education, obviously, because I have some experience there. We have been suffering an energy crisis for years, but our crisis in education dates back further. Education, as you know, is one of the areas where our elected officials have tried to save money in lean tax times. Only a scattered few have understood that cutting education was cutting the lifeblood of our country.

"Health care is another area. We have too much mutual responsibility in that field to let it get any worse. Do you realize that we let people starve and die every day, just to fill the pockets of very rich insurance companies? There are hundreds of thousands of people in this country who are not getting basic health care that we can well afford to give them. That's very close to collective murder, Charlie. And at the very least, it is shooting ourselves in the foot. Sick, uneducated people make for a sick and uneducated population—not to mention the illegal drug traffic that just makes the sickness worse.

"Finally, I think we can change our outlook on world relations. We can meet other people in the world on a different plane and enjoy a lot more understanding in the process. But those are only a few of the points I will bring up during my campaign."

"Mr. Franklin, would you tell us a little bit about yourself and your background?" Gibson was winding up his interview with the typical personal question that everyone would be interested in. He was even more than curious himself.

"I was born Oklahoma City and grew up in Dallas, Texas. From there, I went to a private school in Minnesota, Shattuck School, which is today Shattuck-St. Mary's, and then on to college in New Jersey."

"What college was that?"

"Right here at Princeton University."

"After that, I spent two years in France at the Institute of Political Science in Paris, and then later received my master's and doctorate degrees here. I've taught on the East Coast for many years."

"And your family?"

"I have been married to my lovely wife Susan over here for many years, and sadly, we were not able to have any children. My wife is a psychologist who works in the penal system."

"Do you think that sort of background qualifies you to be president of the United States, Mr. Franklin?" Charlie was trying to put him on the spot.

"Charlie, what are *your* criteria? After all, I meet the requirements set out in the Constitution."

"Well, generally, the chief executive is experienced in other fields, I—"

"Charlie, the people of this country will be able to judge as to the experience and qualifications I bring to the job as they listen to me speak. You, too, may be over impressed by the 'specialization mentality' of modern technology without considering the basic human qualities that make a real democracy work. Why don't we let the banality of your question disappear? If you imply that only certain areas qualify a man to lead, then you automatically believe in a nation of sheep. I don't. I think that there are vast numbers of Americans ready to stand up and be much more responsible than they have been in the past." The answer was firm but not overly dramatic.

About this time, Charlie found a steaming cup of coffee on the table next to him—delicious. He nodded in appreciation to the kind-hearted woman who delivered it to him, Mrs. Franklin. He felt embarrassed and ready to end the interview, a strange feeling for him.

"I guess I'll have to admit that the perfect profile has not been drawn, particularly in light of the choices that we have already made for the men in the Oval Office. Ladies and gentlemen, we have been talking to Dr. George B. Franklin, most recent and very-late-in-the-game candidate for the presidency of the United States. With the two major party conventions just over the horizon, this lone independent, running his campaign on literally no money at all, has thrown his hat in the ring. In the days and weeks to come, we hope to hear more about the details of his platform, but our time is limited tonight.

"It is refreshing to see that someone is courageous enough to defy money, unrealistic as that may appear. And we wish Dr. Franklin the best of luck. Thank you for joining us on the News 12 special report. This is Charlie Gibson. Good night."

As the lights dimmed, Charlie reached for his coffee cup and saw the professor smiling at his closing remarks.

"Charlie." It was the first time he truly let go of addressing the TV host formally. "Do you remember reading the *Essay on Liberty?*"

"Sure, I think, back in college. But I don't remember much of it."

"Well, if you check back a little, you'll find that the author was elected to Parliament in England without giving so much as a single campaign speech."

"Hmmm."

The two continued chatting as the crew packed things up, and Charlie found himself turning a full 180 degrees in his attitude toward the man next to him. He began to like him and respect the strange combination of learning and down-to-earth talk. For a second, he even felt like he had just performed an historic interview.

VI.

"Mr. Stanton? This is George Franklin in Princeton, New Jersey. I hope I'm not calling you too late in the evening."

"No, Professor, not at all. But I'm surprised." How did the stranger know about him? What could the man possibly want?

"This may come as a shock, but I want to make you one of the most outlandish, unheard-of requests you've ever seen. You don't know me, and yet, I want you to take a plane to Newark tomorrow, come to Princeton, and go to work for the people of this country instead of buying them, the way you have done for years. No salary, no campaign budget, and no team. Turn the righteous sentiment of indignation into positive action. What do you say?"

"Taken aback" would be too trite an expression to describe Larry Stanton. Those university educational vibes or ESP wavelengths were doing funny things these days, because he had oddly been thinking of doing just what the man was proposing all afternoon. The two men were destined to be friends, never having met each other.

"I'll be there tomorrow afternoon, but I'll be damned if I know how you figured all this."

"Insight, Larry, is how you bring out other people's good qualities. My insight tells me you have a lot of them."

He hung up and turned off his stereo, right in the middle of the last movement. "Jesus," escaped from his lips as he called the airport. It was about time for an all-out adventure.

VII.

Larry settled back into the somewhat uncomfortable window seat on his just-purchased flight to Newark. As he pondered over the decision, he was amused at his own enthusiasm. Here he was, his name plastered all over the morning papers ("Stanton quits; campaign manager disenchanted"), politely shafting the past, and doing what no one expected him to do. That was probably what made the thrill of adventure drone through his system like the engines of the plane. He was *living*. Little did that screwy world outside know that Larry Stanton was more excited than he had been on the day of his first campaign victory.

This paragon of professional politics was dreaming about how he would help an unknown (totally unknown!) become president of the United States. His computer-like brain was racing down the track faster than the 737, and way off in the corner of his mind, he had an idea that it might work. Everything would depend on the man he was about to meet, but the notion was seductive. It had been coming for a long time, and now somebody had the guts to go out and do it. Moreover, he would be out of the shuffle and jive of dirty, modern tactics, purifying the air around him that had suddenly become so putrid with Milton Wagner. *America loves an underdog,* he thought. This would be the biggest challenge in his life, but the beauty of it all was that he could write the whole thing off if anybody mentioned money. Everything fit. It made sense—in utopia. And Larry's fortune was substantial enough to forget about money anyway.

All through the years, across the eons of ballot returns, Stanton had been selling a product. Hell, someone had even suggested him for director of General Motors. Scads of politicians owed their success to him, probably more than the number of ice cubes at a Washington cocktail party. As he thought about the past, they all looked sick. He knew better than anyone that US politics had become the framework for the oligarchy. "Money pushes the buttons on voting machines" was one of his favorite slogans. No one, up to this point, had disproved him.

But George Franklin (poor Benjamin never managed it, he mused) was out to do just that. The ground rules were simple: no money, no favors, no debts, and no bullshit. He laughed. No bullshit. The childish naivety of it all blew his mind. If you could sell toothpaste, bubble gum, and Cadillacs, then damn it all, you could sell responsibility. And that was one product no one had ever tried. In addition, it prevented cavities—all kinds of cavities. His mind wandered on as the lights of East Coast communities glittered up out of the setting sun.

After checking into the Holiday Inn on the east side of the Princeton campus, Larry whipped out his iPhone and told it to call Franklin's number.

"George Franklin speaking." The voice sounded more formal than it had the previous evening.

"This is Larry Stanton, Mr. Franklin. I've just checked into the Holiday Inn closest to you. When can we get together?" Larry would know after a few minutes whether his trip had really been worth it.

"Get a good night's sleep, Larry. I'll see you in my office at ten o'clock tomorrow morning. You'll have two hours to see whether or not you believe in what I'm doing. If you don't, then stick around New Jersey for a few days and relax. It's a good place to have fun."

Insight—and humor, sure-of-himself humor. It sounded like they were going to have a ball. Plus, Stanton had grown up on the East Coast, so this felt comfortable.

VIII.

Finding his way to the Political Science Department at Princeton University was more of a task than Stanton thought it would be. He found the building quickly enough, but the numbers of the floors in the elevator seemed to have no relationship to the office numbers. Even the diagrams on the walls were hopelessly confusing. "The James Madison Program in American Ideals and Institutions" was on a large placard. He finally arrived, though, and knocked at the professor's door.

"Come in," Stanton thought he heard. Then came a resounding "Come in!"

He walked in, stretched out his hand, and said, "Larry Stanton."

The man who returned his handshake was just as much of a surprise as everything else concerning him up to that point. Vigorous and distinguished, with eyes that were piercing and twinkling at the same time, he beamed the same energy that Larry had felt but couldn't be sure of.

The cubicle-type office was just like the others he had passed on his journey through Corwin Hall, what seemed like a labyrinth of incoherent engineering. Books lined the walls; the shelves were metal, a few papers in disorder, a computer and three-in-one printer, some dust. One refreshing difference from the other offices was the presence of a light-blue rug covering a good part of the drab floor. It made the room come alive.

"Larry, you know the interesting 'twist' of my campaign. No money. But you don't know me. And that's why I asked you to come. If we can accomplish a little communication in the next two hours, I'll be satisfied."

"That's fine with me. Shoot."

"Responsibility, personal responsibility, is the key to making a democracy work. For too long a time, this country has been giving away its sense of responsibility and letting somebody else have it. The examples are too numerous to mention, but why do you think we have such a powerful Mafia in the United States and such a horrible drug problem, fueled by said Mafia? But we—all of us, collectively—sit around and *let* it exist. The prime mover behind my campaign involves getting right down to basics and being gut honest. I intend, Larry, to change the power flow from the vertical to the horizontal, from the top to the bottom. If you want to help me, then you have to be prepared to help Americans stand up for America and each other—and that means standing up and accepting their own individual responsibilities. It most certainly will not mean standing up for me. Does that make any sense?"

"Yes, but won't they be doing that if they stand up for you?"

"Trite bullshit. And I won't delete the word, at least when in private with you. Under present circumstances, that's what you've led people to believe, but it's a game and you know it. What I'm talking about is harder, a whole lot harder. It's turning the game back into reality."

"Just how do you propose going about all this?" Larry was sincerely curious, but with all his experience, he was completely in the dark.

"Attack the public mind, make it hurt, make it vomit in disgust, make it do what you've done with Milt Wagner—and accomplish the whole job with honesty and dignity."

"But how?"

"Simple: just tell the truth, the perhaps painful but honest truth. Historians know that George Washington never cut down a cherry tree. But the underlying moral of the story—paradoxically, its inherent truth—is what survived. The reason is that down deep inside, people *like* truth. It liberates them in a way no pocketbook ever will."

The two talked on until the lunch hour, when Franklin had to meet with someone else. Larry was caught up in the action, however, and would be back for more. He would have to discard old habits, if he was going to work for Franklin. For example, the term "manager" was strictly out. People had to accept the fact they were their own managers, not a flock of sheep to be herded, and that it was high time they acted that way. The electorate was in for a rude awakening. They were used to being buttered up by every Tom, Dick, and Harry who campaigned in front of them. This time, they would have to answer for themselves.

Old campaign slogans, banners, posters, TV ads, and Internet pop-ups were zapped, gone. Wasted energy. No lying, no festering of wounds. This man was trying to point out an obvious truth. The unique thing about the human animal was its wonderful individual differences. Why try to make them think anything else? Why not underline that truism? Respect each other's unique *differences* and you are a long way toward responsible government. Old quotations from Thomas Jefferson were ringing in Larry's head. The point of the campaign was *not to be a campaign*!

As Larry left the office, he was somewhat bewildered—but certain that the trip had been well worth it.

CHAPTER 2

Burgeoning circles of rumor were undulating through Washington at a rate of palpitation that delighted Catherine Nichols. From the not-too-secret tête-à-têtes in well-known bureaucratic night spots to the magnificent, aristocratic cocktail parties in her own mansion, she *breathed* Washington. And since the talk of the town was the scandal in the Democratic Party, Catherine was presently inhaling the Wagner catastrophe.

Mrs. Catherine Nichols was the society person currently in charge (at least as far as *she* was concerned) of social life in the nation's capital. The list of her kind was long, dating back to Dolly Madison, and one might even describe her as a composite of all those charming predecessors. Yet she performed her function in a new and occasionally exciting way. She refused to remain on one level and was constantly widening her sphere of influence—or attraction. She ventured into the political outback, the previously taboo groups, and succeeded miraculously. Because of her widespread popularity, no one dared criticize her eccentricities—not even the Main Line set that came down from Philadelphia.

One example illustrated her uniqueness.

After a lavish party given by the British ambassador, at which her own diamonds sparked in the company of untold coats of arms, Catherine was followed home by a zealous paparazzi/tabloid reporter who suspected her of, shall we say, intrigue. He was almost fooled when an old, battered Volkswagen pulled out of the drive and headed toward a not-too-desirable part of town. A practically unrecognizable Catherine disappeared into the umbrageous epitome of African-American nightlife. The young zealot dared not follow, amazed that she felt safe enough. He noticed that she was dressed in mode blue jeans, her hair straight. A keen eye would have had a hard time distinguishing the "before" and the "after." A few hours later, around two in the morning, the saga ended calmly, and she drove home, dropping the honorable ambassador from Nigeria at his residence.

The story in the tabloid the next day was gilded with trite, uninteresting phrases. It was obvious to the experienced reader that the investigative reporter had buttered up his subject. The woman was his superior in so many respects that he would probably never understand her, even with twenty more years in the business.

Catherine was taking stock of the situation. She, like so many others, had supported Milt Wagner, and she was baffled by the scandal. Oh, she knew he was a crook. They all were. But she, like others, wondered how he could get caught in such a blatant, provable, flauntingly obtuse no-no. He had been around too long for that. Something was fishy. Her feminine intuition told her that, like the Kennedy assassination, this was a put-up job. A mastermind was behind the whole thing, whether they uncovered him now or not. And chances were that the culprit would surface—but when?

Very quickly, though, Catherine returned to the excitement of the moment. All that sensational news buzzing around was a kind of intoxication for her, since, inevitably, they would come and cry on her shoulder. If she had wanted to, Catherine could probably have been the most successful foreign spy in the United States. She had even been approached on two occasions. Unfortunately, the foreign powers in question failed to judge the remarkable woman. She was as loyal to her country as a dog was to its master. The circumstances surrounding her husband's tragic death had proven that. No, Catherine was a socialite—but a very loyal American.

As she mused, her doorbell rang and the butler announced Mr. Wagner. *Speak of the devil,* she thought.

"Hello, Milt." She was considerably less bubbly than the last time she had seen him, but there was still some warmth in the handshake.

"Hi, Catherine. It's kind of you to even let me in the door, given the tornado whirling around me." Surprisingly, Milt appeared almost normal. His late-middle-aged build was robust, with just a little sag in the shoulders. He always wore a gray suit and seemed to have a sad smile on his face, like a masculine Madonna. Not one trace of embarrassment could be seen. He was even philosophical.

The butler served drinks and Milt relaxed in an armchair, crossing his legs.

"What can I do for you, Milt?"

"Listen. That's all. What I have to tell you is going to sound like a weasel trying to get out of a hole, and I don't even understand it fully myself, but there's a catch in the maneuver and you just might get wind of it."

"What do you mean, Milt?" Catherine knew there was something that didn't meet the eye.

"Catherine, the whole story is true, too damned true. I cheated the country out of $2 million in taxes. I didn't do it on purpose; that would obviously have been too incredibly stupid. But I've checked back through the records with a new set of accountants, and everything is perfectly clear. Open-and-shut case. With signatures and the whole bit.

"Now, I don't know whether you've ever done any accounting or even if you've ever filled out the simplest tax returns, but these things are *never* perfect." Catherine, of course, had never so much as thought about either. "Somebody got me, and good. It may take years, or at least months, to find out. Or maybe I really am too old or have Alzheimer's or something. Given the stakes in politics these days, however, I'm convinced there is a very crafty enemy who has been out there for years and who succeeded in destroying me. Anyway, I came over simply to see you and ask that you keep those intelligent eyes and ears open."

"Do you suspect Jack Singleton? He's the obvious one to gain from all of this."

"Hell, no! I've known Jack too long. And what's more, I even had my last remaining friend at the FBI check him out. He's clean as a whistle. No, I think it must be one of the big corporate moguls. They know I would be much more dangerous to them than Singleton. But what's weird is that this thing was planned years ago—that much I do know. It doesn't make sense."

"What do you intend to do, Milt?"

The butler came in with more drinks and put them down on the table. Scotch for Milt and white wine for Catherine.

"Well, what I need to do now, in spite of all this criminal talk, and assuming that I can do anything positive, is keep the power out of the hands of whoever did this. That's another major reason that I came to see you. I'd like to organize some secret meetings, right away, including Jack Singleton, and I'd like *you* to keep the town busy. I know that's asking a lot, Catherine, but I'm hoping that you will say yes."

"How busy?" Catherine had warmed to the sincerity and candor in Milt's voice, detesting him far less than before his arrival.

"A week—or make it five days. Parties every night—"

"I don't know, Milt. How do you expect—"

"Sure, Catherine, it's tough. But I can't think of a better diversion. Bring everybody who is anybody here and let them talk about me all they want. Encourage it, even. But keeping them busy in the evenings and at the cocktail hour is what I'm asking."

Catherine sat back and looked out the window. Did she really want to do this for Milt? Well—yes. She nodded her agreement and bade him farewell. As she watched the gray suit disappear down the walk, her thoughts blurred into the past. This whole picture of Washington crisis was one she had lived before. And a strange, recurrent truth haunted her memories. *They really thought the life of the nation depended on them—and them alone.* It was a beautiful sentiment but so totally false for a woman. If a woman lost a child, she could still reproduce. These people thought the world would come to an end without them. It was so *male*. Her own husband had fallen prey to the same misguided illusions.

William Nichols, now only a name on a family tomb, had been a lifelong diplomat. He was at the height of his career, ambassador to the United Nations, when someone in his office was accused of espionage for China. Nichols was so incensed that he resigned his post and put his reputation on the line. There was a mysterious courier who was never found. The whole affair was on the point of being explained when Nichols, who had told her over and over again that this could *ruin* the image of his country in the eyes of the world, died of a heart attack. Everything quickly quieted down. Catherine remained sure that her husband was right, that his integrity was intact, and she firmly believed in his loyalty. But she knew that, ultimately, he was just a man and that he was far from being so essential, in spite of his many good qualities. It was so damned silly. America was *not* Washington, DC.

The town, though, was her life. Focusing on the present, she called her social secretary and quickly set the wheels in motion. She would give Milt Wagner his five days, and she would stir up as much social hobnobbing as she could. Just wait. She knew, however, that the smoke-filled room where Milt would talk things out with the industrial/military complex and Wall Street would be filled with a bunch of overinflated little boys playing with their egos.

II.

Cadillacs and Mercedes-Benzes began collecting at the Nichols mansion like bees around their hive. A short notice, open-invitation party at her place was enough to arouse the curiosity of more than one member of the Beltway denizen's club. Not to say that they all drove such expensive cars—but the ostentatious rich always came first. Tonight, practically the whole town would be there.

Bradford Jones, the most junior of the juniors in the political arena, felt like he was showing up at the signing of the Treaty of Versailles.

The Wagner fiasco had blown apart the Democratic Party like an atomic bomb. But their bodies were still around to be gawked at.

Brad couldn't care less. He was one of the very few members of Congress who could really call himself an Independent—a registered Independent. His arrival on the Washington scene would have gone completely unnoticed, had it not been for that fact. His constituency had elected him, it appeared, because they liked him. No one could find a better explanation, since his opponent had money and the Democratic machine behind him. His low-key approach to band standing, back slapping, and baby kissing—compared to his blubbering rival—seemed to strike a resonant chord with the electorate.

Of course, the newspapers had picked it up right away. He was a rebel, exemplary of a new trend in American politics, blah, blah, blah. The fact was that Brad Jones was intelligent, strong, outspoken, and enthusiastic—just the right man to be Franklin's running mate, although he didn't yet know it.

His white, fuel-efficient Toyota Prius found a small, empty spot far from the house. Brad checked the door lock, out of habit, and strolled up toward the impressive mansion. He wondered what the legendary Mrs. Nichols would be like in the flesh. On the social side of things, she seemed to be the politician's politician. But to be so successful and popular in such a diverse crowd, Brad reasoned that she had to have some substance. That kind of person could be a powerful friend—or enemy.

A traditionally formal butler opened the door and issued the young congressman, after verifying his identity, into a sumptuous palace. Funny, it even looked like Versailles. The walls of the entryway were covered with mirrors and decorative ornaments that spelled grandeur, authentic antiques. The ceiling seemed to be five times higher than any Brad had seen in the United States. Marble floors, intricate wood paneling, heavy cut-stone fireplaces—Ambassador Nichols hadn't been a diplomat all over the world for nothing, he mused.

Finally, he was introduced to the hostess, after waiting in line behind a few other penguins.

"Mr. Jones—I almost said Mr. Smith—what a pleasure to meet you. For some time, the whole town was talking of your brilliant success, and this is the first time we meet." She was *young*, a million years younger than Brad had expected.

"It is indeed a pleasure, Mrs. Nichols. And thank you for inviting me." Brad was uncomfortable, not so much because of the social atmosphere (one he deplored because of its hypocrisy) but because of the striking woman in front of him. She was disturbing a part of his being that was very personal.

He moved on, letting other arrivals pay their homage, and began to focus on the people as his admiration for the decor subsided. A first! The worst enemies in town were clinking their glasses like old buddies at a school reunion. Brad's sharp eye quickly recognized the ones he loathed the most, the ones who had bilked their government positions beyond the bearable limits. Here they were, wallowing in the disgrace of having duped millions of voters and living off of the fortunes acquired by their blatant dishonesty. They weren't really enemies at all, just loud-mouthed partners in crime.

Where was Singleton? Carlyle? They should be the evening's attractions. He felt a hand on his arm.

"Now that the reception is out of the way, I want to talk to you, Mr. Jones!" Catherine Nichols had singled him out the entire crowd and was paying him what he knew was regal attention. She was apparently out to do a favor to this junior's junior who didn't fit into any traditional mold.

She introduced Brad to many of the most important people in Washington. It seemed like the whole United States House and Senate was there, for starters. Important committee chairs met the underling for the first time. Many of these bigwigs sneered inwardly at his naivety but couldn't help liking his demeanor. And, of course, you never knew when his support might be useful. The fact that Catherine Nichols was paying so much attention to him also piqued their curiosity. Many of the ladies left the party that evening saying, "Doesn't he remind you of that handsome man from South Carolina—what's his name?"

"How do you really feel about the election, Mr. Jones?" She gave him the impression that she actually wanted to know his opinion.

"I'd say Singleton has it now, hands down. Who knows, though; maybe the healthy process of getting rid of crooks will make the public wake up a little more." It was hard for Brad to hide his disgust with Jack Singleton. Of all the rats, Brad thought he was the biggest.

"You think the Democrats will find someone to replace Wagner?" Catherine had already introduced him to five or six possible candidates.

"No. Maybe Plympton. But he won't have a chance."

"Whom will you support, may I ask?" She used correct English, Brad remarked, and that made him smile.

"You may be very surprised when you find out the answer to that question, Mrs. Nichols."

The whole evening was a sounding board for Bradford Jones. Much of what he saw disgusted him (although *not* Catherine Nichols). Inside, he was absorbing the information that would mark his line of conduct. His argument that the Wagner scandal was healthy had raised a few eyebrows and elicited a few comments. No one was offended. They all felt secure, a Washington kind of security, but not one of them owned Brad Jones. They would soon find out how independent he really was—just as Catherine would get an unusual answer to her simple question.

III.

Only a short distance from the Nichols mansion, a few blocks away, in fact, another gathering was taking place. This one was just as lively with conversation but somewhat less festive.

Key members of both major parties (the members missing from the Nichols mansion), who were supposedly traveling outside of Washington, were holding an extraordinary bipartisan get-together. If the general public ever got wind of such a meeting (and what was being discussed), it would spell holy hell for the participants and probably cause an earthquake in the foundations of the two-party system in

America. But both sides agreed that it was necessary. Some way had to be found to diffuse the explosive nature of the scandal and avoid having the general public face the precariousness of the political process. In other words, just like Catherine Nichols said, they actually thought the future of the nation depended on them. The truth, of course, was that the rotten bastards just wanted to save their own skins and stay in power—as many of them as possible.

Most of the people present (not all of whom were politicians) were bitter enemies on the surface and the closest of friends privately, like many of their counterparts at the party nearby. Only this group was one step up on the power plain. They controlled the *real* money, the money nobody ever sees. An uninterested observer might even have taken them for a Friday night poker club—cash on the table. They were all in their shirtsleeves, chatting and drinking Johnny Walker Black Label. General Edgars (chief of staff), Marty Paoli (syndicate numero uno), and Gordon Pearson (CIA) were there, apparently *very* much at home with people they never saw in public. All of the members of this elite group knew perfectly well that they were going to make a "deal," and so they used none of the politically correct jargon their computers fed to their constituents and the public.

Jack Singleton, the next president, was obviously the guest of honor, presiding in an authoritarian way that revealed his real power. When he talked, *everyone*, even Paoli, listened attentively. The pendulum of power was his to swing as he wished, and he could have anyone's head in the room.

Howard Carlyle was conspicuously absent.

"Milt," the older Republican said, puffing some smoke in his direction, "you must make a public avowal, right down to the nasty truth. Throw yourself on the mercy of the nation and tell all. The sooner, the better. If you don't, the snowball will shatter and piss all over you." None of them knew exactly what that meant, but they nodded their approval.

Wagner felt more than a little uncomfortable. He was the one who had helped push this meeting (or so he thought), and he knew in advance that he would have to be a victim. But some of the people present seemed a little too happy to see him cringe. One or two of them had to be behind his fall. Yet he couldn't breathe a word of discontent. The council needed blood. His had to flow. If only he could find out who was behind it all—probably happy man Paoli, the smiling son of a bitch.

"Sorry, Jack. I'm no good at suicide."

"Neither was Nixon, and look where it landed him. You know this isn't personal, Milt. We've been friends for too long a time. We're here in the best interests of the country. Not one of us can forget that. Hell, we all know that billions of dollars flow right through this room. I'm sure you don't want to see a breakdown of the whole system in the morning."

"No, Jack. You're right. Just give me time enough to figure out the best way. My wife and kids will have to be sheltered in some way, but I'll do what the group wants."

The discussion then exploded into a thousand different suggestions, some of them absurd. Most of them wound up admitting that the next few days of news coverage would lead them to a consensus of some kind and that Wagner would probably do some jail time.

As Milt was walking to the nondescript car he had parked three blocks away (in the opposite direction of the Nichols mansion), he thought he saw a small shadow skirting the back fence of the home where this first meeting had just taken place. Probably some kid who lived in the neighborhood, or maybe a cat. Pearson had handled security, so he had no fears about whether or not any part of the meeting had been overheard. No. If it had been a person, it was somebody authorized to be there. But the shadow was so short; it probably was a cat. Milt started his car and headed home, forgetting to fasten his seat belt amid all the drama raging in his head.

As he muttered to himself behind the wheel, Milt wondered whether it wasn't all stupid. The future of a metal worker in Pennsylvania and a housewife in Arizona, was it really in their hands? The strength of the nation's institutions was supposed to be far greater than the individuals who occupied elected offices. All of them should be expendable overnight. But the very means they had used to acquire power and the devastating psychological effect of succeeding over and over again had overshadowed such a fundamental truth. Those poor men were convinced that the fate of America rocked precariously on their shoulders. And it was true that so many people had been lulled into accepting their hypocrisy. Did that mean that the "people" were basically stupid and uninformed? Informing them now might be the best way to confuse the poor souls. What had life come to?

As he sped down the last street (Milt was a fast driver), which was lined with trees, a powerful red laser light ignited and blinded him. He instinctively swerved to the right and disintegrated against a tree, disrupting the symmetry and continuity of the *ordine lignorum*.

Milt Wagner had just committed suicide.

A small, dark figure with a thin smile and a handheld device like a pen calmly poured a bottle of Johnny Walker Black Label on the burning corpse and watched the alcohol add to the flames. He hopped up into a waiting Mercedes. It drove away very slowly as lights came on like Christmas trees in the neighboring homes.

CHAPTER 3

The blue rug in the Professor Franklin's office, hardly ever vacuumed, was generally graced by the presence of students or fellow faculty members and showed the coffee stains of numerous academic *causeries*. Unlike most of his colleagues, he kept his door almost always open. He had risen in the ranks largely because of it. And the number of influential books he had published rivaled the scholarly reputations of his most well-known colleagues. He was highly respected and appreciated.

From the very beginning of his career, George had a hard time with the expression "publish or perish." He had a passion for teaching and thought that a really good teacher would automatically spawn interesting questions from the students—and that many of those questions would need investigation before they could be answered. So he had pretty much assumed that good research evolved from good teaching, at least to a certain extent. Early on, he found out that even the most prestigious institutions only gave lip service to good teaching. The best way to get skipped over for a raise or a promotion was to spend too much time with the students and take the time to nurture their interest in learning. And no one seemed very concerned about the blatant failure of secondary education. Treating students like animals being herded through a system—that's what he observed. And he couldn't do it. The element that boosted him to the top was his passion for answering those questions. He was one of those rare individuals who needed very little sleep. And if people could have interviewed Susan, they would have heard countless tales of her finding him up in the middle of the night writing and doing research.

The interplay of discussing and searching was George's bag. He liked human beings and couldn't hide the fact. Most of the students, undergraduates and higher, who invested time to know him felt at ease dropping in at any time. They could talk about political faux pas, American politics, or switch to Medieval French literature, Business French, love affairs, or Art History, Philosophy, Horticulture—you name it. Needless to say, the famous, world-renowned intellectual giants who lined the same corridor in Corwin Hall wondered how he managed to perform at such a prolific level. Some of them were a little jealous.

It went without saying that George enjoyed enormous popularity among the students. His classes were always full, cracking at the seams. Under the guise of liberal policies, he forged more work product out of them than most of his colleagues. The simple fact was that they *liked* it. And everyone knows that when work is not considered as work, you like it. When he announced to his classes, for example, that there would be no final exam, because he didn't believe in final exams, they shouted for joy. One less all-nighter at the end of the semester. That made the writing of an original, twenty-page paper sound so much more palatable. Even the subject of the paper was not imposed, though he wanted to discuss it individually with every one of them. The idea was to develop something that had aroused their curiosity, either because of class discussions or their readings. Of course, the long hours they spent working on it were far more than they would ever have committed to preparing for a final exam. Learning the tools of research in the library, the time spent discussing the project with Franklin, the multiple revisions—all of those things had become *fun!*

Then, too, his attitude in class was different. He seemed to be talking to equals, or, at least, he wasn't talking down to inferiors. He had a pleasant way of emphasizing one point in three different ways. He was a comedian, delighted when he could make them laugh. All in all, the man was adored—but not completely understood. He was about three or four steps ahead of them all the time.

Many of his good friends wondered where George found the time to read about all the stuff he knew. Talk was fine, but you had to get the info from someplace. What they didn't see was that Franklin, like Benjamin, in addition to his midnight research, devoured all the books he could get his hands on. In addition, he was a successful speed-reader, at about a thousand words per minute, with 90 percent retention. This was something he never talked about, hiding it carefully behind a veil of discreet silence.

The students were possibly the least surprised, but they were a little taken aback when George made his declaration for the presidency. No one really considered him to be a political activist. In almost all of his discussions, he appeared to be conservative on some points, liberal on others, and occasionally radical. No discernible political pattern. He never took part in political rallies or functions. Never spoke out much in public. Hardly ever stopped to listen to a good old political harangue on Cannon Green.

He had been known to do some out-of-the-ordinary things. Declaring his salary insufficient early in his career, he had done all sorts of outside jobs to supplement his income. And he was always very open about that to the university. Since his evaluations were always excellent, there wasn't much they could say. But that period of economic necessity didn't last long. He and Susan soon made enough money to live comfortably. And that's all they wanted.

One of these attempts to earn some extra cash early in his career turned out to be profitable. He wrote a series of children's books with a friend in New York (who received all the credit; George only earned a percentage of the royalties). They were aimed at four- and five-year-olds, and each one had a message: don't go out after dark, clean up when you're finished playing, be kind to animals, etc. They were fairly well received and gave him a little income for a few years, but the older professors and his department chair looked down their noses at such a silly waste of time. Franklin's argument that it was impossible to enjoy life and hobbies for a hundred dollars less than that of a Trenton garbage collector fell on deaf ears. Later, as he became published and received tenure, he wrote political science books that were well received at colleges and universities around the country.

The higher you went up the academic ladder, the more you heard, "George Franklin as president of the United States? Oh my God!"

II.

The phone on George's cluttered desk gave a decisive, administrative-sounding ring. Sure enough, it was the dean's office.

"Professor Franklin?"

"Yes?"

"Dean Watkins would like to talk to you," the administrative assistant droned, like one of those digital voices on an answering machine.

"Fine. I've been expecting his call." George knew that the higher echelons of the Princeton pyramid would be sufficiently disturbed to take some kind of action. He also assumed that their public relations office had received more than a few calls.

"Professor Franklin? This is Urban Watkins. I'm calling to talk to you about this business of running for political office. Is it true?" Watkins didn't need to ask the question, but he had to get the conversation going somehow.

"You know very well it is, Urban." George took a keen pleasure in being very informal with these bigwigs.

"Well, we're a little surprised here in the administration, since we didn't get any advanced notice from you. I've had calls all morning, frankly. You're quite serious? This isn't some kind of publicity stunt or classroom lesson?" He sounded just a little belligerent.

"Quit beating around the bush, Urban. If you have something to say, say it."

"I don't need to remind you that, Dr. Franklin, this campus has a reputation for political activism that dates way back, and we don't need another era of riots and tear gas. Furthermore, I think it's my duty to inform you that the facilities you occupy in Corwin Hall cannot be turned into a campaign headquarters. This is all really very disturbing—"

George was not about to be stopped by a mere university official.

"Urb, take a hard look at what's going on in this country—in the world, for that matter—and even in this university. You scratch the surface and then dig a little bit underneath and you'll find some basic problems that need solving—now! Then, listen to what I have to say about the solutions. *After* you've done that, call me again. In fact, I'll go one better. Cancel whatever luncheon engagement you may have and let me set you straight today."

"Well, I—" Urban Watkins couldn't seem to find the words to express the frustration in his voice, but his tone was doing an adequate job of communicating it.

"What do you say, Urban? Let's hash this out together."

"All right. All right. I might as well get it from the horse's mouth before the president and the whole damned board of trustees fall on my head."

Urban Watkins was a tough-sounding but basically soft customer, one of those top-notch researchers turned lousy administrator. On his way to a Nobel Prize in plant adaptation and protein research, Urban had been jerked out of his brilliant career and stuffed into an office where he had to hire and fire secretaries, among other trivial duties. He had agreed to all of that, which made some of the faculty question just how far along he was toward that Nobel Prize, but on the surface, it looked like he had given up on his mental curiosity and opted for a steady six-digit income.

Urban was a nice man, like a nice New Jersey day. So he remained dean. They even decided to keep him for longer than the normal five-year hitch. Everyone who wanted something at the university had to see Urban Watkins. And he had grown accustomed to the power.

The two men met halfway between their respective buildings and headed toward the Faculty Club. As they were strolling along, Urban remembered the days when you could take the same walk and see an odd mixture of everything from a long-haired hippie to a mod dresser. On a day like this years ago, you could experience song and sunshine and ranting and raving at the same time. In the shade of a small tree, you might have heard two bearded violin players bowing a Vivaldi favorite, filling you with the rich tones of their instruments, expertly rendered. And then, a little farther on, a pickup group of guitarists and singers, swaying to some Bob Dylan tune. And then, a few steps farther, you could have run into the harsh sounds of a heckler blending in with the screams of some religious fanatics. *Those were the days*, Urban thought, when all of that fit together in a paradoxical harmony. Was this professor an image out of the past?

The dean quickly reverted, however, to his bad mood, glowering and biting his lip, as though he were afraid to speak his mind (good administrators *never* do). But he managed to come out with some trivial small talk until they settled at their tables in the Faculty Club, near a window that still painted the nostalgic picture in Urban's mind.

Then, Urban blurted out, "Okay, let's have it!"

"What do you mean?

"Come on, Franklin, just spit it out and let's get this over with." Urban had decided to continue playing the power trip.

"Urban, one of the realities of any citizen's life, but perhaps more so of a teacher's, is to balance personal responsibilities and civic responsibilities. The latter have had a tendency to be overlooked today, and it is time to focus on them. For a multitude of reasons, our country has been taken away from its people. It is time to give it back. Or at the very least, it is time for us to talk about that."

"What do you mean?"

"I'm out to put things into a different perspective. One of the major themes of my campaign is going to be a challenging of *everybody*. The power structure, including you, by the way, is acting as though it doesn't have to answer to anyone anymore. Transparency is a spin word. There is nothing that is transparent. While that structure manipulates in ways that are frighteningly reminiscent of dictators, creating fear in the hearts of the masses, it has castrated or disemboweled its constituents—or so it thinks. For example, do you consider yourself a servant? Your salary is paid by the university. But down deep in your heart, do you pay any attention to that? You know perfectly well that most of the meetings you attend on this campus are, by university standards, supposed to be transparent, but you treat them as if they were a little too private. And the reason you do that is simple. You have detached yourself from the reality of your democracy. I want you to get back to it."

George didn't sound like a fanatic. He wasn't raving. He was hitting Urban where it hurt. Instead of worrying about faculty, students, and personnel for the last few years as a lackey for the administration, the man could probably have saved millions of lives with his research. He knew damned well that the comfortable salary, combined with his ego, had drawn him into a comfortable rut of malfunction. It was oblivious to the public that he was supposed to be serving. He probably never even thought about them.

"Just what the hell are you saying?"

"That it's time to be honest and responsible, not warped and insouciant and egocentric, Urban."

Franklin was just warming up.

"You sit on a silly throne. You know damned well that your effectiveness in this academic institution is running at about 10 percent. You haven't published a single thing in the last four years, which means that you are no longer setting the example for the people who have. Nor have you taught a class in that time. You're about as far removed from the meat of academia, the classroom and the students and the library, as I am from the moon. And you know in your heart that I'm telling you the *truth*. But that truth hurts so much that you sweep it under the rug. And yet, you live as though you knew what was going on in education. You have meetings and you form committees and you *masturbate your brain* in a world of hypocrisy. Urban, you're not responsible."

"Now, listen here—"

"Urban, you know very well that overt, obvious, stinking policies—some of which you have personally implemented—are the very last to get changed, for the very simple reason that they are so overt, obvious, and stinking. The system in which you are operating does not know how to deal with embarrassment—another word would be out-right *failure*. Hell, man, you need to start doing what I've been doing in my classes since day one—get rid of your inhibitions!"

Dean Watkins sat back and frowned a little deeper. This wasn't the first time that a professor had cried injustice and wrongdoing. And ordinarily, he would have just smoked his pipe and smiled benevolently. Just one of the lower-downs that was angry about not being on the road to promotion. But here was a new and ominous twist. If this ever became part of even a mildly successful presidential campaign (assuming, of course, that this upstart made it to first base), it had the possibility of becoming a migraine. And the horrible thought mulling around in his mind was that this man Franklin was ... right. Like the social elite of Washington, the people with power on their side felt delightfully secure, full of pat excuses for ignoring the truth, ignoring the truth, ignoring the truth.

"I think you should probably talk to the president. We're all quite aware of what you're saying, Franklin. And I think you will be surprised to see what's being done about it." Urban was trying to save face.

George Franklin smiled. Watkins had learned a little about politics after all.

"I'd love to talk to the president. In fact, there's a good chance that we'll have a public debate."

Watkins squirmed in his chair. *Oh my God! We're going back to the seventies!*

III.

When George returned to his office, he heard the phone ringing from a few steps away. Not his cell phone. He picked the receiver up just before it was going to switch over to his voice mail.

"This is George Franklin."

"Dr. Franklin. Listen carefully. Senator Wagner was murdered last night. I said *murdered*. I have proof. Good-bye." The caller hung up.

George looked at the phone and frowned. He took out a small notebook from the only locked drawer in his desk and jotted down a few lines: date, time, exact words, masculine voice, young, no particular regional accent, maybe a tinge of Michigan or Wisconsin. He replaced the notebook carefully, locked the drawer, and put the key away.

IV.

The afternoon was still full of work. Professor Franklin had his class to give. He was going to lecture on Montaigne's *Essay on Education* (Urban Watkins would do well to read it) and was well prepared for the barrage of student questions about his move into politics. For the most part, they were bright, intelligent kids—sharp as tacks.

He walked into the classroom a few minutes early and was immediately besieged by a crowd of waiting students. "Are you really running for the presidency? Is it a joke?" George just nodded and went up to the podium for his lecture/discussion. He wove the French philosopher's message into his fifty-minute presentation and finished the class on what he thought was a high note. As they crowded around him again, George said that he would love to stay and chat but that he had some pressing business. He hoped they understood, which they did. But he did need to speak to one of the students privately.

Jimmy Weeks, editor of the *Daily Princetonian*, was one of his best students. Medium-length hair, open shirt, blue jeans, casual—Weeks was special. He didn't go after the grade, and only the grade, like many of the others. Weeks was the kind of person Franklin wanted to encourage, the responsible kind of element he wanted to awaken throughout the country.

"Jimmy, I want you to interview me for the *Daily Princetonian*."

"I was going to anyway. Sounds far out, the no-money business and everything. Right on. What's the story?" Jimmy didn't need a pad and pencil—and hidden behind his California jargon and mildly sloppy appearance was a very perceptive mind.

"No payola. No bullshit. I want to get the people of this country off their asses and get them to work together before it's too late." The professor could speak Jimmy's language.

"Do you want to make that a direct quote?" Jimmy laughed.

"Whatever you think is good journalism. The point is simple: quit talking and do something."

"What's your stand on illegal drugs—marijuana, heroin, coke, ecstasy?" Weeks would ask his own questions.

"Opposed to anything that smacks of avoiding responsibility. You buy illegal drugs and you put a ton of money into the hands of some very bad people, people who would cut your mother up in little pieces and leave them on your doorstep if they didn't like you. You buy illegal drugs on a black market with no taxes and you put the burden of dealing with the consequences—sickness and addiction-related crimes—on your fellow citizens. Egotistical and irresponsible. You want illegal drugs, go out and get enough people to vote for legalizing them. As simple as that. Responsible democracy."

"Affirmative action? Racial equality? Diversity?" Jimmy's eyes were piercing.

"The complexity of our society is one of its beauties. Different races, different religions, different political convictions—difference all over the place. And the one thing that every person in our society can do is decide to respect and honor that difference, not fight to destroy it. How do we do that? We channel our energies into human understanding—and I don't mean that in a religious sense. We focus on human dignity. That requires calm reflection and restraint and acceptance, even admiration for difference. Once that hurdle is crossed, once we have admitted that truth to ourselves, we will have the groundwork laid for improvement, drastic improvement in the fiber of our society. Until we move in that direction, the wounds and anger and abuses will fester even more than they are now. That's why money cannot be a part of my campaign."

Jimmy Weeks was beginning to pay closer attention. He had been turned off by the marijuana bit. His generation considered it no more dangerous than candy. But he hadn't done a lot of thinking about the flow of money. And now that he did, he painfully realized that there were probably American military personnel being killed with funds that had actually come out of America from the sale of illegal drugs. But he wasn't through digging.

"How do you expect to bring about this moral upheaval and revolution? Sounds like you want to be a new Jesus Christ."

"Nope. I want people like you, if you think there's anything to what I'm saying, to *act*." George walked over to the door and made sure it was closed. He lowered his voice and continued. "And I want every chapter of the Underground Student Activists to challenge my ideas until they are blue in the face. If they can't find a loophole, then by God, I want them to get this show on the road."

Weeks was flabbergasted. He lost his cool. The very fact that Franklin had uttered those words sent chills up his spine.

"How the hell did you know about the USA?" Their network was tighter and more security-conscious than Osama Bin Laden's had been. And it operated on 73 percent of the campuses in America, and was growing daily, in large part due to the power of the Internet and encryption of e-mails. They had avoided publicity like the plague. If Franklin knew any details, he was one very well-informed—and potentially dangerous—man.

"No secret. I talk to a lot of students and know how to put two and two together. Insight, if you will, plus a keen interest in what you're doing. I know that you are at the top of the organization. If you'll continue to listen to what I have to say and follow up with a nationwide debate on the inside, you'll have a far greater impact than the article you intend to write for the *Daily Princetonian*."

Shit! thought Jimmy. This was scary. The interview had turned into a top-secret conference. After two hours of political rambling and theory, Jimmy came away with some ideas that would blow the organization's mind. Tactics and strategy had been applied haphazardly on the local level by every chapter for the past three years—the main theme being the power of the student voice in America. Their success was virtually unknown but surprisingly effective on a number of issues. Lacing through their makeup was, of course, a certain level of maturity. Jimmy himself had sensed this from the start. Yet, this apparently mild and learned professor of "political science" (an oxymoron, Jimmy thought) was pointing them in the right direction. He decided to convene a general meeting of the chapter leaders and spell out the program of "responsibility." The generation gap was, after all, bullshit, to a certain extent. That would require some convincing. But any mass movement of political importance in the United States had to include the young and the old, the rich and the poor, everybody. The weakest links and the strong ones had to join forces, not fight or be frightened of each other.

They talked about freedom and liberty in a new light. You had to impose considerable limits and restrictions upon yourself in order to be free. Doing anything you simply *wanted* to do was not liberty. Jimmy was doing some growing up himself.

As he sat down to his keyboard to finish his story for the *Daily Princetonian* that evening, Jimmy decided that he would go all out— kind of like Franklin picking up the phone and calling the AP. He would support the most unsupportable candidate in the history of American politics. To hell with the far left, to hell with the smaller issues, to hell with sticking up his middle finger at the post baby boomers. He would drum up support—nationwide support—for George Franklin.

CHAPTER 4

As a growing number of diverse supporters started to rally around Franklin, the campaign came alive. Their variety went far beyond people like Larry Stanton, Charlie Gibson, and Jimmy Weeks. They included folks who generally had nothing at all to do with politics. This leader, or hero, or whatever he was, corresponded to new criteria that were emerging from the masses—an expression of deep-seeded concerns surfacing after years of silence. Professor Franklin seemed to appeal like Roosevelt had, stimulating a desire to participate instead of waiting around for things to happen. Gibson's original broadcast had received an unprecedented series of inquiries and created a snowball of follow-up coverage from other stations. The people who wrote in wanted to see more of this unusual candidate. Volunteers were sending e-mails from all over the nation. Somewhere behind the lethargy of modern American voters, a strain of latent civic "responsibility" had been found. Gibson had come out of retirement.

It was really no surprise. The past few years had been too much. Scandals both in and out of the government had disgusted practically everyone. America was involved in overseas wars that did not really make sense to most Americans. Young men and women were dying or being maimed for life. The economy was going downhill. People found themselves in front of two politicians who didn't have one iota of *real* support. No matter how successfully those two (now only one, after the Wagner debacle) managed government, their underlying weakness and corruption, gnawed at the guts of the common man. And that common man was now to be reckoned with. Franklin began to look like a catalyst. His base of support expanded as the news spread.

These were not people who waved flags and jumped up and down to loud band music while their candidate passed out slogan buttons. They were not automatons of the already-existing political machines that rang doorbells, attended political meetings, and formed popularity clubs. And they were obviously not big businessmen who tied their own interests to the bandwagon of a puppet. No. They were citizens who felt the same pain of ultimate shame that Larry Stanton and Charlie Gibson had felt. Like them, these people were waking up after years of passivity. Those years had been spent assuming that what they had learned in grade school and from their parents about democracy was true and that their government would be honorable and truthful and good. But they were quickly losing faith, particularly when they filled out their income-tax returns. Now, after all those years, someone was convincing them that they could do something about their destiny and that money was not necessarily going to rule them. They were throwing off complacency. A phenomenon, rising out of their own numbers, might revitalize America beyond their wildest dreams. It was worth a shot.

Other politicians had kindled similar fires in the past, but their time had not been ripe enough. Perhaps the rapid pace of economic and technological growth had left them wondering how that could possibly keep up with mass communication techniques. Perhaps they had felt incapable of standing up and being heard—lost in the crowd. Whatever the explanation, they were coming out of the woodwork now. Franklin's message of strong, simple human values and dignity was filling the vacuum, turning the tide. A large segment of the American population was waking up. And the traditional politicians touting "change" had no idea what was coming.

Decadence, if it could be called that, was transforming itself and following a new curve—no longer downward.

As the campaign developed, an unusual series of events began to occur in the two major parties. Jack Singleton and his Washington cohorts had worked out an interesting compromise that seemed to correspond to what *they* believed reflected the nation's needs. The body politic was now in no mood to elect a Congress and a president that would be at each other's throats all the time. And the way things were shaping up, it looked like a possibility. So, out of their smoke-filled rooms arose some not-so-strange bedfellows.

Observers, particularly European observers, had known for years that there was no basic difference between and a Republican and a Democrat. As one recent visitor remarked, "They are like two rival clubs." After some mildly heated discussions, more for the pleasure of dispute than anything else, the two clubs decided to join forces—excluding, naturally, the undesirable elements. In short, the election would be rigged again, but with no slipups this time. Jack Singleton would be president, but in a sweeping bipartisan gesture, he would appoint numerous *highly qualified* Democrats to key positions. This would create good feelings in the majority, appease the populace, and, most important of all, maintain the status quo. All very neat.

And for a while, the plan worked admirably well, amazingly well. Jack, good old Jack, began to weave a few conciliatory remarks into his speeches and weed out the scandal-mongering. In addition, he developed a healthy, work-it-out-together line aimed at preparing the public for *new* politics, a little like some new kind of toothpaste.

No one apparently had given any thought to the possibility of failure and least of all to the possibility of competition, under the circumstances. As the weeks went by and as the summer conventions approached, it was only with mild curiosity that anyone noted that this Professor Franklin was appearing in the polls. Condescendingly, they decided that they had to show some impartiality. The newcomer's attention, generated solely by the press, made a few people talk. But they chalked it up to the novelty of the no-money thing, firmly convinced that America would never take an unknown element like that seriously.

Here was a person who thought he could become president of the

United States without so much as a single campaign poster, much less the backing of a political party. No headquarters, no funding, no media spots, no blogs—no nothing. Just a bunch of garble about democracy and "responsibility." Hell, *they* were democracy, and nobody was going to change that, not in this world. It was a proven fact that if the stockholders in major corporations really decided to participate in meetings and vote for directors, the entire economy of the world would collapse. And had *that* happened? Forget it.

II.

Only one person in Washington was paying close attention to the inch-by-inch progress of Dr. Franklin: Brad Jones. He listened to every broadcast and every interview, taping them. He read every article he could find about the man. He couldn't get enough.

To each of these reports, Brad applied his own rigid standards and beliefs to the rhetoric he charted. And faultlessly, time and time again, the two fit like a glove. On a national scale, this professor was trying to accomplish, single-handedly, exactly what Brad wanted to accomplish in his much smaller sphere of influence. Nowhere did he feel the slightest negative vibration. He was constantly amazed by the growing coverage this man was getting in the news. He thought it was the most positive sign of a wake-up call he had ever seen.

Washington was in for the surprise of its life. Brad Jones, popular himself to a certain degree, was going to support Franklin for the presidency. They had never met, but their ideas automatically brought them together.

Ordinarily, no one in town would notice the impending change. But Catherine Nichols had a sixth sense. She had taken a liking to the young congressman during that first evening and had included him in all of the subsequent get-togethers. Quick to notice his mention of the unusual professor, she uncovered more than just a passing interest. Of course, Catherine was devoted to her own games, playing the friendship and tragedy of Milt Wagner to the hilt, yet, she couldn't

JOHN C. BEDNAR

help sympathizing inside with the obvious rejection of all the superficiality she herself had created. That haunting dream of years gone by was lying under the surface, gnawing at her social façade. And she couldn't get Milt's visit and death out of her mind. Somebody had to get rid of this power-hungry crowd that was ready, apparently, to kill to stay in control. She hadn't believed for one minute in the ruling of his death as an accident.

One day, she asked Brad, "Why do you talk about that professor all the time?" The fact was that he hardly ever mentioned the man, but Catherine's intuition was better than ESP.

"He has his finger on the real pulse of the nation, the heartbeat. He is saying what many Americans have wanted to hear for a long time. They know that they have been controlled by money interests. Many have been cajoled or coerced into accepting what is good for the money people, not necessarily for them. They want, deep down, to fight back. But they have never seen any way of doing it. If Franklin is elected, he will do more good for the country than this entire collective body." He waved his arm toward the Capitol dome.

"You can't really *believe* that. He doesn't have any experience."

"No? He may not have any *Washington* experience, but it sure sounds like he has some very positive *life* experience. He pushes the buttons of civic action—in a way that I've never seen before. I know it sounds corny, but he's waking up the good side, to use his words, the *responsible* side. That is a very powerful force."

Catherine thought for a minute. It was such a gratifying dream. Yes, the Beltway crowd was playing a game. But no one had ever *changed* it. It was almost like cheating and lying and stealing from the taxpayers was a foregone conclusion. And the funny thing was that many of them had come to Washington with honorable intentions and high standards. And not long after they began there, they succumbed to the corruption. They were overwhelmed by it. They weren't *bad* people, just weak. How many times had she listened to the old adage, "Does the man make the office or the office the man?" The answer was traditionally that the office made the man. But what if the offices themselves were corrupted, destroyed by a force that had long ago set out to destroy them? If someone could rejuvenate, revive the meaning of these offices, make them *responsible* again, then maybe the good would be able to resurface. *Star Wars*, she thought. Wow! Brad had provoked a dream that she thought she had buried long ago.

When Brad arrived at his house that night, he sat down to write a letter—and thought a lot about Catherine Nichols.

III.

"George?" Larry had only recently become comfortable using the man's first name, in spite of the strong feeling of comradeship between them.

"Who the hell is gonna be your vice president?" After all this time working like a dog, the supreme political specialist had forgotten all about the structure of his own government! *That will have to go into my scrapbook,* thought Larry.

"Good question. I was wondering when you would ask." There was a twinkle in the professor's eyes. "He's a newcomer, kind of like me. Clean, idealistic—he has already bucked the odds by getting elected. Of all the people I've followed, he is more capable of turning the vice presidency into a real leadership position than anyone else."

"You *cannot* mean Brad Jones." The smile on George's face broadened. "You *do* mean Brad Jones!" A second's reflection made it clear. *Of course, stupid me,* thought Larry. Brad Jones was the perfect candidate. He was one of the few defeats Larry had suffered, albeit indirectly, while working for the Democratic Machine. Something had gone wrong. The whole thing had been blamed (by him, of course) on misinformation bubbling up from subordinates who didn't know what they were doing. Far be it from Larry to admit, at the time, that he had been super careless about an Independent. The vague memory in his mind was that he had ironically admired the guy back then.

The phone rang.

"George Franklin??"

"It's for you." Larry handed the receiver over to George.

"George Franklin speaking."

"Hello, Dr. Franklin? This is Bradford Jones calling from Washington. You probably don't know anything about me. I'm a junior congressman from—"

"Mr. Jones, I certainly do know something about you," George interrupted. "You are one of the few elected representatives of the American people that I consider to be very *responsible*. You come from a small congressional district filled with some of the finest and most courageous people in this country. They chose you instead of money. Tell me something: How would you like to be my running mate in this election campaign?"

Larry's mouth was hanging wide open as he witnessed what he could only describe as a self-fulfilling prophecy. Well, goddamn! Talk about coincidences. And Brad's jaw had dropped an inch on the other end.

The call went on and on. Open and unfettered communication, agreed-upon coordination, adherence to the zero campaign budget and how they would handle that, the rebirth of democratic spirit—and a million other things.

As Larry overheard the Franklin half of the conversation—George did not put it on speakerphone, though he did tell Brad that Larry was standing next to him—he was again surprised for the umpteenth time. He was discovering a hitherto unrevealed body of knowledge on the part of his candidate. Nowhere had he seen political publications, in Franklin's office or at home, yet the man knew one hell of a lot about congressional matters. He knew the names of obscure representatives whose names were almost never in the news, their voting records, and even bits of information about their personalities and characters. When it came to pinpointing their stands on issues, he invariably measured them against his own yardstick of *responsibility*. Larry was blown away. *He* was familiar with political machinations and their microcosms! But he had spent a lifetime acquiring it, paying attention to it. How had an obscure professor of *political science* acquired it? What the heck was going on here?

It was a foregone conclusion that Brad would accept the offer. That is why he had called. The letter, now torn up in front of him, was addressed to Franklin. The two men, side by side, would conduct their campaign in exactly the same way, hammering out the theme of the public itself being the key element in the success of any democracy. Oddly enough, both men knew perfectly well that this was an adventure like none other. It wasn't going to be easy. And that made them both all the more committed.

The respect they had for each other was obvious from the first few words of their conversation. And it was filled with *humility* on both ends. Larry Stanton found himself wondering why in the world this hadn't happened before.

In some ways, though, it had. Throughout the entire history of the United States, there were numerous examples of democracy functioning as it should, individuals rising to the greatness of their human potential. The unsung heroes of American life were there, giving their full measure and then fading back into history. They were part and parcel of the backbone of the nation, doing what they were supposed to do, guaranteeing the freedom of others either to be *responsible* or not.

Brad Jones was of that ilk. And when the phone call ended, Larry Stanton knew it.

IV.

Convention time was around the corner and Dr. Franklin was beginning to upset one prognostication after another—to the dismay of more than one convention delegate. So many people were talking about "the man without a party," and it made them nervous.

No one knew who suggested it first—and in all probability, it came simultaneously from various parts of the land—but Franklin's name was bubbling up from the ranks of countless districts in *both* parties. True, he was registered in neither camp. True, they had already been committed to their first votes through the primaries. But many of them

JOHN C. BEDNAR

were thinking, *That man should be our candidate!* It was disturbing, to say the least.

Apparently, the peregrinations of the American political scene, particularly the financial structure, had been bothering many a soul long before George Franklin appeared. It just didn't seem right that a person with good ideas, a strong character and leadership qualities, couldn't become elected without money. Somewhere in the hearts of hundreds of thousands of new supporters for the professor, there was a mixture of traditional puritanism and sympathy for, or identification with, the underdog.

This was naturally very disturbing to the leaders of the political machine. They knew that the doorbell punchers were vitally import-ant, no matter what modern electrical communication could do. Yet try as they might to sell their candidates to the public with money, they had to admit that this year's crop of puppets was sadly mediocre—more mediocre than usual. They all lacked the charisma that this outsider Franklin seemed to have. So, eventually, some of them began to listen to the ground swell of discontent.

If the guy's popularity continued to grow, why not make him a dark horse in one of the conventions? It had been done before. Split the ballots so wide on the first few votes that it would look like no one candidate emerged, and then "Bang!" pop Franklin into the flood-lights. Even in the Republican Party, where Jack Singleton looked like the only man in town, many of the delegates secretly felt like he was an incompetent old buzzard. He was feared by a few but not a popular choice.

The first person to take any action was Walter Barber, who ran the Democratic Machine in upstate New York. Larry Stanton had worked closely with him in years past, and Stanton's about-face had caught his attention. After a couple of telephone calls with his old cohort, he suggested Franklin in one of his strategy sessions. Naively thinking that this was his own brainchild, Walter threw it on the table. To his utter surprise, everyone agreed.

Miles away in Wisconsin, Arthur Swenson made the same suggestion to a group of undecided Republicans. By the end of the meeting, they were drafting a letter to Franklin expressing their support in no uncertain terms.

Similar actions were cropping up all over the United States. He was a good man. Darn it! What he said made sense! Why should so much money be spent on trivial amusement? It was about time they found a candidate who was interested in and maintained confidence in the social fiber of the country. And since Franklin was a political virgin, at least insofar as anyone knew, his image could withstand the brutal and vicious personal attacks that had become so commonplace in modern politics. He was Jack the Giant Killer, a hero, a David against Goliath. They could play up that theme and sell the man as great—enhancing the party's power in the process.

So, in one week, the Franklin household was bombarded. Telephone calls, e-mails, people ringing at his door, all of them saying, "How about joining our party?"

The neighbors must have been particularly impressed by the presence of four black limousines in the street on one sunny afternoon in Princeton. They would have laughed their heads off had they witnessed the Hollywood comedy going on inside. The governor of New Jersey, a leading senator, a mayor from the Midwest, and another bigwig were begging the man to join up with them. It looked like a bunch of NFL football execs vying for the number-one football draftee.

To all of these overtures, the professor remained polite but firm. It was simply out of the question. Had they had their ears closed before showing up?

Finally, one of the brightest recruiters pointed out what he thought would be a decisive argument, blue in the face after trying everything else. How, he said, did the man expect to have his name printed, electronically or otherwise, on the millions of ballots in November, if he was not the representative of some party? It simply would not be in front of their eyes when they went to push the buttons or pull the levers on the voting machines.

Franklin sat back in his chair and smiled a broad smile, a humorous glitter in his eyes, while his interlocutor, red in the face, gloated. He looked the man straight in his shining pupils and said, "A citizen who votes is a person who goes through the sacred act of putting his confidence in another human being. If the people of the United States really want me to be their president, they will have to be so certain of their choice that they write my name on the ballot. In fact, I won't accept any other kind of vote." And he took a pen from his pocket, punctuating the remark with a gesture, writing his name in thin air.

The statement was repeated on his next television interview, thanks to Charlie Gibson, and the polls instantly went up three points.

George took out his secret notebook and jotted down the following line: "Signed ballots in the national archives for public inspection?"

CHAPTER 5

Charlie Gibson had grown even more in stature with his colleagues since his decision to come out of retirement and interview Dr. Franklin. Gibson had endeared himself anew to the nation. His name was plastered all over the United States. The tape had been shown countless times and translated in forty-three languages around the world. And naturally, he had received quite a few new job offers, even from large networks. But Charlie was happy to be retired and would have nothing to do with them. He was so wrapped up in the no-money crusade that they even made him laugh. And he wasn't the only one. This new idealism was a spark to hundreds of media people who secretly had felt the same way for a long time. They wanted to be free from the shackles of commercialism. "Freedom of the press" had become a trite catchphrase, a meaningless piece of drivel. They were tired of prostituting themselves for years before they could graduate to the glorious pinnacle of "integrity."

It was an unexpected opportunity. The fire for simple truth was burning—and no one knew exactly why. Franklin had received offers of so many bribes; if he would just show up in a studio and say something somebody wanted him to say—bribes worth literally millions. Franklin just laughed. Not one dime was accepted and they were all thrown out on the street. In addition, the offers were made public. The castle of cards came tumbling down. The man meant what he said. The money-grubbing press was coming across as just what it was: self-serving and stupid.

The gauntlet was thrown down. The national press had rarely been upstaged and revealed for what it was. Franklin and his volunteer team were hitting where it hurt, uncovering the seedy side of the news. And the result was beginning to show up all over the country. Strict orders about news content were being disobeyed by rebellious newscasters. Large advertising backers were befuddled by a renegade group of reporters who started refusing perks—the payola that had kept them in line for so long. Their employers, part of the problem, who were subsequently coerced into muscling their rebellious news people, were blown out of the saddle when a middle finger shot in their direction.

"What the hell is going on? Don't you know that I'm the fiddler and you're paid to play the tune *I* want? *None* of us will have jobs if the advertisers pull out!" This was the attitude of the large execs.

But it didn't take. And it didn't even take up the line. Many execs joined the bandwagon. The chairman of New Jersey News 12 (a newly acquired friend of Charlie Gibson) actually spit back in the face of one his advertisers, "Every second of your future advertising will go on the air the way *we* want it to go on. If you don't like that, too bad!" He went on to point out in more polite language that his broadcasting system had a responsibility to the American people that was far greater than his responsibility to an advertiser—and that if they were called upon to bait the American public with lies, they would simply not do it. The news was not going to be manipulated for money.

Well, Mr. Merchandiser dropped his cigar in his lap—in an uncomfortable spot.

After years of creating false sensationalism, the press could not change overnight. But the courageous decision by Gibson and others to take a stand against materialism's immoral pressure on the truth was a resounding signal, quickly echoed nationwide. In relatively short order, serious voids occurred in the cash flow. Products ceased to be sold, because they didn't appear on the screen amid murders and sensational kidnappings. Advertisers were going crazy.

The local news had been stagnant for some time. Up until Charlie Gibson's adventure, though, their image was overshadowed by the big networks. Cultural programs and ad-less newscasts took a backseat to sensationalism. Little by little, that started to change. Professor Franklin was adamant about refusing donations, and many of his growing supporters understood that a free press—not manipulated by money—advanced his cause.

As a result, nonprofit community television stations felt a shot in the arm. Charitable contributions came their way. Obviously, the general public was no longer buying what they had previously been sold. It was a movement by thousands of people who wanted to rid themselves of a common disease. Miracle of all miracles! Public TV was becoming popular!

Nielsen ratings started going crazy. Corporate America, at least insofar as television advertising was concerned, was in a quandary. Sales fell off during the lag time for them to understand what was going on. When they finally understood, they were quick to react. Some of the biggest advertisers moved toward whole movies or shows with advertising only at the beginning or at the end, like in Europe. "We want *you* to enjoy an hour and a half of uninterrupted pleasure." And the effect was positive all the way around. The public quit being pissed off about advertising and even left the channel button alone at the end of a program. Sales did *not* decline but even went up a little. This was not a bad move.

When concentration is constantly interrupted, it has a tendency to destroy equilibrium. As more and more people found themselves enjoying their television time, they also became calmer and more reflective. In short, the boob tube started doing them some good. This subtle revolution was weird. Television started contributing to their cultural existence.

II.

"Hello, Larry? This is Charlie Gibson. Tell me, could I pick your technical brain for a minute?" The two were working closely together now, and Larry proved to be a continual source of practical knowledge.

"Sure, what's up?"

"Well, we have a little problem. The battle with advertisers is pretty much a thing of the past. But political money, and I mean one heck of a lot of it, is doing its best to sabotage the principles those folks pretend to support." The alliteration of his s sounds punctuated his own convictions.

"What exactly do you mean?" Larry thought he had a fairly good idea of what Charlie was going to say.

"They're trying to dig up dirt and buying time to put it on the air. It's about the smallest pile of dirt I've ever seen, and I'm assuming that Franklin will turn it into gold, but I'm a little worried. Do you know of any way to get our information out faster than they can?"

A pause in the conversations showed that Larry was thinking.

"You have to counterbalance with the whole truth—and nothing but. Do you know when they've scheduled the spots?"

"We have a fairly comprehensive list."

"Then get to work on the newsmen closest to them. The more open and objective everyone is facing any given circumstance, the better. Only people generally aren't open and objective, they're close-minded and afraid. That's what this whole campaign is about: waking people up to the truth. If the opposition is intent on closing their minds, we have to beat them at their own game. Just one difference— we must do it honestly. You know, if you play games too often with the electorate, you can get roasted."

Both men were showing a tendency to fall back into old habits, reasoning the way experience had taught them. Franklin had pushed them more than once right into the fallacy of their thinking. He played philosophical hardball. For Franklin, the ends simply did not justify the means. He pointed out that you could do just about anything you wanted to in the United States if you had money. Money was the explanation for everything, an easy way of avoiding responsibility. But watch out. If the *people* ever decided to stand up and say that they had had enough, no amount of money in the world could stop them from wiping out what they abhorred. Benito Mussolini, after all, had been hung up by his heels. Meaningful human action is backed up by something stronger than materialism.

Franklin was absolutely right. By speaking openly about any and every bit of material brought to the public's attention, he would simply be following his ideals. A brisk "darn it" escaped Charlie's lips as he thought about how easy it was to get back into the very mold from his past that he was trying to break. He sat down at his computer and started banging out a cold account of the trifling bit of smut the opposition was drumming up.

III.

To Charlie's surprise, many of his colleagues had already been writing up similar accounts. The whole to-do was about Franklin having studied for a couple of years in France and people trying to imply that he was morally suspect like Hollande, the president of France.

"Do *you* want somebody like that to become president?" That's what was being put on the air. Charlie watched News 12's airing.

> "Jack Singleton, the front-runner in the race for the presidency, has approved of a series of television shorts that appear to darken his own prospects more than those of the candidate he is attacking. His staff has apparently been trying to discover skeletons in the closet of Princeton professor George Franklin, acting on the belief that there must be some dirt somewhere. They have come up with what this reporter considers to be one of the weakest smears in the history of this sort of thing.
>
> "Here are the accusations. Professor Franklin did graduate work in France and became influenced by President Hollande, who has had four children with a woman without ever marrying her, insinuating that Franklin might have the same morals. And they have

found *one* student who says that he is intimidating as a professor.

"The people of this country will undoubtedly take exception to the un-thought-out jibes that refer to Professor's Franklin's student years at one of the world's most prestigious institutes of political studies, particularly when they learn that he was not a student there at the same time as Hollande.

"And we have managed to interview the student, who stands by his statement that Franklin is intimidating in class. When we asked him, however, to elaborate, he said that the television ads had taken everything out of context. He actually said that he *liked* the way Franklin was in his face and made him participate in class. The intimidation, he said, was positive.

"When we add to this development the fact that Franklin has received the university's coveted Distinguished Teaching Award for two years in a row, it makes Singleton look foolish. Perhaps the most significant aspect of this news is that it exists at all. If a senior member of the United States Senate can stoop to such a widespread smear campaign on such flimsy grounds, it is a sure sign that the man from Princeton is on his way to being a viable candidate in this year's crazy election."

As he listened, Charlie realized how true the analysis was. It was nothing short of amazing that the leading candidate, Jack Singleton, would authorize the use of such banal material if he weren't scared of the professor. Talk about blowing your mind! This series of stupid ads was the first solid evidence that Franklin was in the race. There was, after all, no substantiated dirt in these ads at all. They were doing more to promote Franklin than harm him.

JOHN C. BEDNAR

IV.

"Carlyle!" Jack called him Carlyle when he was in a bad mood. "What in the name of merry hell went wrong?" It never occurred to the senator that he should have been asking himself this question, but for once, he had given some rope to his campaign manager and was convinced that the subordinate was at fault.

"I don't know, Jack. It looks like you read signs incorrectly. I'm telling you, this professor represents something that can't be dealt with using our old weapons. It's like a wave, or a movement or something. Hell, I don't know."

"Did you send the order out to cut the shorts pronto?" he asked, not realizing that this was the fourth time he'd made the request.

"Sure, but the moneymen are pissed off. It'll take a little doing to make up for the loss." Howard wasn't really worried about cash, but he thought his comment would shock the discussion back into the realm of practicality.

Jack Singleton was in a mood that would upset anyone. Like a male hippopotamus fueled by testosterone, he was running on angry. The deep wrinkles in his brow betrayed a cloudy, disturbed spirit. Something was eating away at the man, something more than the tactical error he had just committed. He knew how stupid it had been to instigate the smear campaign, and he felt incapacitated by the mistake. How could he have failed to size up the situation, particularly since he had done it so successfully in the past? He was stymied. There was something weird going on and he was losing his touch. But more than that, he felt the pain of how downright asinine he had been. This professor, this goddamned university professor (who didn't look like the other pseudo-intellectual pricks *he* had known) was too pure, too *American*, and the son of a bitch was *right*. Absolutely everything the man said was the embodiment of the same clichés and principles they had all used to get elected. The only difference was that he *meant* them!

As a professional politician, Jack didn't like to think the things he was thinking. He kept repeating to himself that the golden rule of political success depended upon a person's ability *not* to think that way. But, damn it, he was convinced deep down inside that this charismatic character was accomplishing more already than most of them had spent a lifetime preaching about. He thought back to a conversation he had had with the ambassador to India when the Senate was considering types of foreign aid. The ambassador had just come from learning of India's mission to the United Nations, where the problems of improving the lives of millions of poor people, living in ghetto conditions, were hotly debated. Technological and scientific education initiatives were proving their worth, and outsourcing of jobs to India was constantly on the rise. But they seemed to be more preoccupied with the *human* side of the equation. Many of the Indian representatives were convinced that improving a man's outlook, improving the quality of his spirit, would act like a catalyst and rub off on the other members of a suffering group. Sure, more and better housing was fine, along with improved medical care and especially food—but all of that was a waste if you didn't do anything about the inner self.

And that's what Franklin was doing. He was going to the heart of real problems and suggesting human solutions. After all, money was just a lot of green paper that didn't mean one silly thing until it became the logical extension of an attitude—rather than convoluted thinking by Singleton. And there they were, at the top of the pinnacle, convinced that the allocation of funds would somehow be able to buy the right solution.

Regaining his senses, Jack said, "Howard, what do you really think of this guy?" He took out his bottle of eighteen-year-old single-malt scotch and filled a tumbler. He usually didn't ask Howard Carlyle about anything.

"I don't know," that's what he *always* said, "but I can see signs of his changing the way we do politics. He has created some pretty major upheavals in the way I see reporters doing television and radio, and even the advertising industry seems to be influenced. Do you realize that I sat down last night and watched *Law and Order* from beginning to end without a commercial? And it was regular programming, not a

DVD. They put all of the ad time at the end. Now, Jack, *that's* a major change. If we don't look out, he might get elected." A cloud appeared over Jack's uninterested face. "You know, you could make use of some of his ideas when you move into the White House. It wouldn't hurt your image at all."

The two men continued chatting. They finally agreed that they had over exaggerated the importance, the practical importance, of Franklin's campaign. Stealing some of his ideas and using them as November approached would put them just that much further ahead. Their underlying admiration for some of what the man was saying had probably caused the unwarranted fear that sparked those stupid shorts on TV. A simple, tactical error that could be repaired. They knew very well that, attractive as it might be, revolutionary as this fellow's campaign might appear, he didn't have a prayer of being elected. It was just too far-fetched to take seriously. No. They were confident in the thought that Jack could start looking around for the best speechwriter in their camp to compose his inaugural address. He was sure to win.

V.

Back in New Jersey, Fox News was conducting an interview with Franklin on the Princeton campus. It was a beautiful day, and the large stone buildings seemed to reflect some of those old precepts of knowledge that the institution was supposed to represent. They were sitting outside on a bench in front of the Faculty Club, overlooking the rose garden that had inspired the same scene close to the White House.

"Professor Franklin, what importance do you attach to the criticism raised by Senator Singleton concerning your having been associated with the French president?" the reporter asked.

"Well, as you have already learned, we weren't students there at the same time. And responsible Americans learned a long time ago that guilt by association is basically unfounded."

"Do you think that your ties with France and your fluency in the language will in any way affect your campaign negatively?"

"On the contrary, I think they will help me to communicate better with all of the French speaking countries in the world, in Europe and Africa. And by the way, Americans learning foreign languages and being involved in foreign-exchange programs around the world can only enhance our abilities to communicate globally."

"Could you comment on the student who said you were intimidating?"

"I thought it was a totally fair comment. I *am* intimidating in many ways. And I hope that the people around me will be intimidating, or at least willing to speak their minds openly, to challenge. That student, by the way, is exactly what students ought to be, ready to stand up and say what he thinks and defend his position. The fact that he appreciated my aggressiveness is irrelevant. *I* appreciate his. He isn't jelly. He has substance. Aren't we all supposed to be like that?"

"Do you think that you have lived up to the highest standards of teaching?"

"Good grief, no!"

"Could you comment?"

"You are using a superlative. It's impossible to live up to the highest standards of teaching, or anything else. What's important is that you try. In government, for example, I get the impression that too many of us have quit trying. We let ourselves be ruled and swayed by promises—when we know that the promises are lies."

Franklin paused a minute and then continued.

"In education, to get back to your question, we have created too many pressures to do things other than teach. The tenure system, instead of protecting academic freedom, has become a destroyer of human beings. I'm dead serious. And people who can no longer be honest with themselves are people who cannot further the principles of education. In government, it's the same way."

"What would you propose as a solution to these problems?"

"There isn't any one *solution*. All of the people in the whole country are at fault. One proposal that I think might help is an educational system uniformly recognized throughout the nation, with high standards maintained and controlled."

"How would nationalized education help?" The interviewer was genuinely puzzled.

"The pain in the side of our educational system is its inequality. A nationalized structure would have a tendency to make the system more homogeneous and therefore less discriminating and unfair. This is particularly true today at the lower levels, where you have problems of adaptation and a lack of common goals. But behind most of the problems in education, whether a nationalized system is adopted or not, there is the underlying problem of attitudes. We must commit ourselves to education before anything can really be done. And I think all Americans know this and want a better future for their children."

Franklin seemed to become more passionate.

"You know, we live in one of the few countries in the world that has nothing in its constitution about education. As a society, as a collective whole, we have embraced the concept of free public education for all, but we constantly withdraw our support when the economy turns sour. The people who say that their taxes shouldn't go to educate the poor people in some community thousands of miles away are wrong—dead wrong. They know very well that the quality of instruction in the whole country, if it is good, will improve their lot as well. But local monetary reasoning prevails.

"In the concept of compulsory education, everyone seems to have understood the word *compulsory* but not the word *education*. So many of our schools in large cities have become little more than prisons or babysitting institutions. And we wonder why there is so much violence. Did you know that more than 15 percent of the high school graduates in our country are functional illiterates?"

Now he was really getting fired up.

"That situation is a sin. It is a social sin. By allowing 15 percent of the high school graduates in large urban centers to be functional illiterates, we are denying them the very rights and freedoms that our

Constitution guarantees. By closing off their minds, we are making slaves out of them—sheep to be slaughtered."

The interviewer tried to get a word in.

"Is that the fault of the system, or perhaps the result of the social ills prevailing in our society?"

"Both, of course. We have created an environment in which individuals have the freedom to be sheep. But by refusing to care about them and by continually *diminishing* the quality of the public education they receive, we blithely condemn them to a squalor, both mental and physical, that only becomes a greater burden later on. Ideally, we should have a system with high standards and results, capable of dealing with all the heterogeneous problems—and that system should be completely free and completely equal all over the country. According to their capabilities and interests, students should be able to go straight through from kindergarten to their doctorates without paying a cent for education."

"But how do you propose to pay for all that?"

"You put it at the top of your priority list! Our current priorities could easily be rearranged. We do not need to be spending the incredible amounts we spend on destroying human beings as opposed to bettering their lives. Why, the energy we devote to the creation and maintaining of weapons of mass destruction, for example, is mind-boggling! No, this nation can decide to organize its ledger sheet in a much more humane way."

"If we could move to another topic, Dr. Franklin—you have mentioned health care as an important area that needs attention. What would you propose as an improvement in health care?"

"The same thing: nationally funded health care, particularly in the area of prevention. Our neglect of this other factor concerning the well-being of our citizens is scandalous."

"Could you elaborate, please?"

"The quality of medical care, when it is available, is both high and expensive in our country. There are many ways that we can reduce cost and increase availability."

"How?"

"One of the very first ways—harping on the theme of my entire campaign—is to become much more *responsible* for our own health and the health of our children. Look around you. We have an epidemic of obesity. We are almost all overweight, and every day, we eat millions of tons of food that is not very good for us. Now, changing that requires the same sort of self-discipline that any other responsibility requires—and it doesn't cost a thing. In fact, just some mild restraint in the area of gorging ourselves with harmful and unneeded calories would represent a savings to every American family that would blow your mind. On the front end, there would be more money in a family's monthly budget. On the back end, a decrease in the incidence of diabetes would save us billions in medical bills later on. And this is just one area. If you go down the list of things we could do on our own to improve our health, you would find more than enough savings to fund wonderful health care for everyone."

"That's asking for a lot of self-discipline that doesn't seem to exist, Dr. Franklin. Otherwise, we would have seen it already, because most of the population is aware of the excesses and bad food habits you mentioned."

"Well, that's my point, isn't it? No one voting for me in this election should think for one minute that I'm going to avoid telling them the truth or keep from pointing out the choices they are going to have to stand up and make—for themselves and for their country. And those choices are going to involve a lot of courage, the courage to do what is right. If that starts happening, you will not only see universal health care; you will see insurance rates going *down* because there will be fewer claims, and you will see our prison population diminish radically. People can decide, you know, not to commit crimes!"

"Dr. Franklin, our time is up. We would like to thank you for this interview and remind our viewers that this broadcast has been presented in the public interest at our own expense. No payment of any kind has occurred between Fox News and Dr. Franklin. Thank you."

V.

The lips of a thin smile closed in silence as a small, impish figure deliberately squeezed the "power" button on his remote. He sat back and stared at the ceiling as his mechanical smile turned into a frown.

CHAPTER 6

Catherine Nichols looked out the window of her Volkswagen and wished she could speed along faster on the freeway into downtown Washington. She was on her way to a rendezvous with Brad Jones and was dressed much differently than she had been at their first meeting. Simple clothes and a simple hairdo reflected her mood. Brad, now that he was an official candidate for the vice presidency, represented an ever-greater source of curiosity than he had before. More than that, he had awakened feelings inside of her, suppressed for so many years since the death of her husband.

Fortunately, for the moment, there were no other Milt Wagner's calling on her to manipulate Washington society for the Democratic Party. Everything seemed to have calmed down overnight. Of course, she knew that this meant compromise and secret solutions. And she wondered a little about what the party was going to do. But she was slowly forgetting all that. Brad Jones, unperturbed and confident, was more exciting than the social whirl she had long considered her lifeblood. There was something about the man that announced a new game. Since her party, he had grown in everyone's esteem, but it was mixed with fear. She was reminded of the jealousies she had seen in more than one pair of eyes. The uneasy feeling, only barely discernable on the surface, was one of wariness. He was an iconoclast, breaking the images reflected in the Potomac, but he was doing it in such a nice way. What was she really feeling?

As she parked in front of his apartment building, she noticed a group of reporters leaving through the glass doors. They looked anxious, impatient to get their copy written. They didn't look tired and disgusted, the way she had seen them so often. One of the fellows recognized her and waved his hand, a curious look on his face.

She walked up to the intercom system and pushed the button next to Brad's name.

"Yes, who is it?"

"Catherine Nichols, Mr. Jones."

The buzzer hummed and she pushed the door open and walked to the elevator. A tiny janitor, dressed in blue work clothes, was washing the marble floor, swishing his mop back and forth in small, even circles.

"Hello, Brad," she said as he opened the door to the small flat.

Bradford Jones was a bachelor, and his living quarters showed that a woman had not done the arranging of the small amount of living space he occupied. The most prominent kind of furniture in the living room was shelving, all over the place. And they were filled with books—Shakespeare, Plato, Aristotle.

Pausing to look at the titles, Catherine said, "I didn't know you were so literary. You and Professor Franklin obviously have more than one thing in common."

"Oh, those are just companions. Some people like to do other things. Guess I'm one of the weirdos who read."

Brad was discreet about his private life. Catherine had noticed that right from the beginning. From what she had been able to learn, he had lost his fiancée in a tragic accident. A graduating medical student, she was about to begin her internship in a Harlem hospital. On the very first night at work, she had tried to get some information out of the hospital archives in the basement. The irate husband of the librarian came screaming into the room with a revolver in his hand and started shooting at his wife. Brad's beloved caught a .22-caliber bullet in the neck. She remained on the critical list for three weeks. The vigil next to her deathbed had drained him, marking him for life.

But years had passed since that tragic event, and Catherine wondered whether he might not be ready to live again, just like herself.

"What can I offer you?"

"Anything. Hope you'll excuse my outfit. I suppose you know that I don't always conform to the traditional dress code." Catherine really felt very much at ease.

"Yes. I've heard a few stories about your escapades. But I'm much more interested in you as a person. And I was very grateful for your kind introductions to Washington society, boring as it is."

"You have some pretty strong convictions about Washington and the country in general. They seem to be echoed everywhere all of a sudden. Lot of talk going on!"

Brad handed her a glass and sat down on the sofa opposite her chair. He didn't look at all nervous and certainly didn't exude the impression of thinking of himself as a future vice president. He was about as normal as he could be.

"Looks like you have the answer to your question. I'm going to support Franklin to the hilt."

"Won't that ruin your brilliant young career?" Catherine was deliberately testing him.

"Maybe, but I'm convinced that politics shouldn't be a business."

"Do you really think it might work?"

"That will be up to the people. They decide whom they want. But that's a pat answer. The voters who write our names on a ballot are going to do it because they *really* want to. In a way I think that those signatures, no matter how many there are, will have a special meaning attached to them."

"The odds are about a million to one against you, maybe more. You know that." The tone in Catherine's voice left Brad with the impression that she was saying what she thought was the gospel truth, but that she didn't want it to be that way.

"I'm convinced that if Americans wake up and get involved, they will vote for Franklin. Oh, I know that what we're saying sounds impossible. It really would be mind-boggling, wouldn't it? But people can change if they are motivated, and Franklin is doing that every day. I mean, what could sound like a more utopian dream? But you know, Americans have done a lot of utopia-creating when they have set their minds to it. They have a reserve of energy, desire, and self-discipline that is hard to match anywhere on the planet. Mark my words, if you think the little spark of interest you see today is something, wait until November!"

He was full on conviction. Young, robust, a little foolhardy, timorous. But there was a resilient maturity behind it all. They were about the same age.

"Listen, Brad, this may sound strange to you, since I've been so involved in what you might call the opposition, but … what can I do to help?" Her question raised the image of Milt Wagner in her own mind, and for a fleeting moment, she wondered why she had uttered this incredible sentence. It just sort of came out.

"Help break the barrier." Brad was looking at her with powerful eyes, staring straight down inside her soul.

"All the way?" she said, incapable of turning her eyes away.

"Yep. All the way." He grasped her hand and applied just enough pressure to show that he meant what he said—and maybe more.

Catherine hesitated for a minute, taking in the reality of what was going on. She knew what he meant. He wanted her to abandon the world she had fabricated so deftly for so long, the reputation she had acquired. She would have to stop playing a social game and let her inner convictions replace her heretofore superficial existence. That was all very well and good for a man—but a widow? Something in his look threw another element into the fray. She leaned over and spontaneously kissed him.

"Okay, Brad, I will. I simply will!" She stood up and smiled, filled with much more than enthusiasm for politics, and stared once again into those eyes. "America, here I come!"

II.

Catherine nudged her Volkswagen back onto the freeway with a strange feeling of importance and elation. It wasn't at all like the thrill of Washington intrigue that had been her daily mantra for years. It was more like the calm understanding that had illuminated the first years of her marriage. She suddenly pictured herself in the midst of hostile eyes accusing her of betrayal—and she liked it!

As the trees flew by and she passed the endless condominiums of suburban Washington, Catherine thought of the odd circumstances surrounding her conversion. It was a comedy that brought home the truth of her existence, a laughable portrait spilled onto her mind. No one, absolutely no one, would understand. But she didn't care. She was not only going to support Franklin and Jones; she just might be Mrs. Jones before it was all over!

The garage door closed behind her, and the electric "click" of the lock drew her attention for the first time since it had been installed. Funny, she thought, how so many people come home to the same sound.

The comfortable wealth that Mrs. Nichols enjoyed was, during this period of osmosis, taking on a new air. It would be some time before the society people realized exactly what was happening, but that was all right. Slowly but surely, this paragon of social acceptance was leaving her past behind. Ever so diplomatically, she was becoming politically important, really important, for the first time in her life. No strange actions, no overt statements, rather a serene understanding, a tranquil self-confidence, obliterated the veneer.

This permeating effect went beyond simple conversation. It fore-shadowed a drastic change. No longer would the mavens of Connecticut Avenue be at ease. When they came to sip her champagne and enjoy her hospitality, a strange whiff of danger met them at the door. The "salon" of game-playing seemed cheap and out of place. Even the merriest revelers who returned to their cars after the parties wondered how different the evening had been. Their baffled minds sensed change and challenge. And from Catherine Nichols!

Many a senator or congressman went home ill at ease after an evening at Catherine's. They were like animals who sensed they were about to be killed, stalked by an unknown predator—on their way to extinction.

III.

Since Professor Franklin's campaign was now much more than a humorous comment on *The Situation Room* newscast, Wolf felt obliged to interview the candidate whom he had initially presented to the public—as a joke. He decided to call the professor's residence directly and set up the time and place.

"Hello? Professor Franklin? This is Wolf Blitzer calling from New York." The voice sounded calm and somewhat tired but filled with the professional sincerity that had always been part of his psyche.

"Hi, Wolf. I kind of figured you'd call after you tried to make a joke out of me and it turned out to be a real news item." It was George's turn to joke around. The two had both attended eastern institutions at different times, but they had roomed with each other during a conference on international relations. He knew that he would not get any stupid questions from Wolf.

"George, I did some checking on your Princeton days and found out a lot. You apparently had quite a rebellious spirit. Now that you've received a lot more attention, I'm doing my job, pretty much what you're saying we should all do. The network has assured me that it will provide the necessary setup at its own expense. There will be no violation of your money policy."

"You know that you don't need to apologize, Wolf, and I'll be happy to talk with you as long as you want. When would you like to come out here, or do you want to set things up through your affiliate here?" The question was asked with no particular tone. George knew that they did "live" interviews from all over the world and could make them look like they were side by side.

"If you're free, I thought we could set it up for day after tomorrow.

Our people here in the city will be in touch later today to talk about the practical details. I'm looking forward to grilling you." Wolf laughed the warm laugh that had endeared him to millions.

"That's fine with me. Good to hear your voice—and by the way, I know a little something about your college days as well."

IV.

As luck would have it, the sun was bathing the Garden State in a way that had probably influenced the folks who decided to call it that so many years ago. The camera crew arrived in the morning and had everything set up for a midday interview.

The place they had chosen was a wooden deck behind the house, surrounded by a small garden in full bloom. Large oak trees towered in the background, hiding a small brook. They had placed two non-descript chairs on the scene. Although the setting was far from the magnificence of the White House lawn, it was somehow reminiscent of the famous interviews with Kennedy that Cronkite had conducted so many years ago. Charlie Gibson, who was present as an observer and knew Wolf Blitzer, noted the comparison on a slip of paper as they were starting the interview.

Blitzer began, his familiar voice attracting the attention of half the country.

"Dr. Franklin, your candidacy for the presidency has become a phenomenal grassroots movement throughout the United States during the past few months. Many people are wondering just how all of this came about. Do you think there is any chance that you have created a trend that will last?"

"I certainly hope that increased participation in the democratic process will continue. It's the key to a meaningful future. But I don't credit myself with an act of *creation*. The people who are supporting my candidacy are asserting *themselves*, and they know full well that they are stepping forward to work harder in the process. Sweeping changes in the way Americans decide to live—less waste in all areas and particularly in the area of energy consumption; less crime, more attention to personal health and preventive medicine; elimination of the illegal drug traffic; compassion for the sick and needy, just to name a few—those changes will be the result of people assuming *responsibility* for their acts. And it is far from promising an easy street. It will be hard." His earnest voice showed that this last comment was not a political ploy but a sincere conviction.

"Do you honestly think that it is possible for your candidacy to lead you to the White House?" Wolf knew his listeners would want this question asked.

"Yes, or I wouldn't be campaigning, if you can call it that."

"If that happened, it would stand out as a unique phenomenon in the history of the United States. No one has even come close to doing this. A candidate with no campaign funds, no precinct workers, no banners or slogans, and no party affiliation would occupy the highest office in the land on a *write-in* ballot! In our day and age, if such a miracle should come to pass, what would you do as your first presidential act?"

"Diffuse the inordinate amount of political goodwill accompanying that sort of mandate and remind everyone in the country that they would *all* now have to step up to the plate and do *their* part." He pronounced these words slowly and deliberately, looking directly into the lens of the camera trained on his face.

"What do you mean?" Wolf seemed genuinely puzzled.

"Obviously, Wolf, the miracle, as you call it, would invest an extraordinary amount of power in the hands of the president because of its huge break from tradition. Under the present framework, the balance of power that has been so precious in our political history could be unsettling, making an already powerful office too powerful."

He paused.

"But the people who vote for me are expressing a totally different mandate, almost the opposite. They will be voting for leadership and responsibility at all levels of government, right down to themselves. To modify a phrase made popular by Truman: 'The buck is *not* going to stop with me.' Those bucks are going to stop with the people who are much further down in the system. In short, I fully intend to *decrease* the power of the presidency. And I hope the Congress of the United States will follow my lead."

It was surprising, even to Wolf Blitzer, who had heard a lot over the years.

"What, if anything, do you propose to change in the field of foreign affairs?" Wolf was moving to one of his favorite subjects.

"Aside from a much greater amount of cultural and educational exchange, particularly among young citizens, there is one area of the Foreign Service that I can tell you right now I would change: the way in which ambassadors are appointed, or at least some of them. Career diplomats will get the nod, not big campaign contributors, mainly because there won't be any. The ones who bought their way into the job will be out, right away."

"Most of us are assuming, Dr. Franklin," Wolf couldn't hit on the right name to call him, "that relations with France would be high on your priority list." Wolf was smiling.

George returned the smile, but his eyes showed some concern.

"Like I've already said in another interview, I hope I will be able to improve communications with all of the French-speaking peoples in the world, but if you think for one minute that my former professional and personal ties to France will create any favoritism, you don't have much confidence in my own sense of responsibility. We all inhabit the planet together, and we all must shoulder our own burdens. My priority is the United States."

Both men gave the impression of being perfectly at ease as they talked. Candor and maturity dominated the conversation. Charlie Gibson was impressed. George Franklin seemed worldly all of a sudden. His demeanor was aging in front of Charlie's eyes.

"Professor Franklin, you have spoken at some length about education and health care, suggesting many changes that are considered as socialistic in nature, such as the nationwide educational system and a possible broadening of the role played by Social Security. Do you really think the general public will support these measures?"

"The serious-minded and responsible public will support programs that improve the quality of all the lives of our citizens. Being creatures of habit, we have a tendency to be wary of change. But if we honestly examine the waste, inefficiency, and low performance of these systems, we should step up and make them better, much better. We should forge ahead and look for solutions. But in the final analysis, it is very difficult to solve problems with methods or structures. Human problems must be solved by human beings, working together, working and being compassionate."

He continued.

"For example, when I say that education should be free through college and graduate school, I don't mean to imply that the recipients of that education do not need to reciprocate. That is my very point. Their education will automatically lead them to giving back some of what they have received. Educated people become aware of the world around them. It is the greatest form of wealth in the world. And it will be shared."

Wolf decided that it was time to wind up the interview.

"In all the years that I've been reporting, Dr. Franklin, I have never seen a political candidate more doomed to failure. The *realities* of modern politics all go against you. The odds of you being elected are not much better than the odds of winning the lottery. But you may be teaching us an important lesson here. This discussion has been interesting, and I leave you with the feeling that it would nice if you could win. Thank you."

Wolf Blitzer, without knowing it, had very professionally just pinpointed the reaction of the millions of people who would be watching his broadcast.

V.

No cuts had been made of the filming, unless it was the choice of takes from one of the two cameras. It would go out almost unedited on the news, except for shortening long pauses to save a few seconds on the air. When he reviewed it, it reminded Wolf of some famous interview in the past, maybe one of Jack Kennedy. The dignified, charismatic charm of the man from Princeton came through to him in the same way. Many of the close-ups, zooming in on a look or an expression, continued to draw the comparison in his mind. Charlie Gibson had made the same comment to him, but it was only now that he really saw the parallel.

Wolf knew that he was giving George Franklin more time on the air than he should, but he did it anyway. A couple of his team members pointed this out, but Blitzer held fast. The message was strong enough for him to put his reputation behind the decision.

When he wrapped up the final newscast, having catapulted Franklin into a much brighter limelight, Wolf felt good. He picked up the phone and called Charlie Gibson. For some reason, he just wanted to chat with him.

CHAPTER 7

The twenty-first of June, first day of summer, longest day of the year, also announced the beginning of the Democratic Convention. Many of the delegates probably wished that the daylight would go away sooner, so they could escape into the cover of darkness. That was the fun time of day anyway, and no one was enthusiastic.

A splinter group seemed to lurk in the corner of every committee room, arguing about everything. The disappearance of Milt Wagner had opened up a Pandora's Box of opinions. Favorite sons were embarrassingly plentiful and relying on their constituencies to put their names forward. All of a sudden, the whole dad-gum party was eligible, and most of them wanted to throw their hats in the ring.

The pandemonium of discord filled the convention hall, to the delight of the reporters covering the event. Everyone knew that the nomination would go to a dark horse. That's all they had!

But the wiser old coots that had been around for a very long time soon injected some words of wisdom. They argued that instead of worrying about any particular individual, they should concentrate on finding a prototype capable of *defeating* Singleton. Few, if any, were aware of the secret meetings in Washington. These few always voted against whatever proposal was made. So, slowly, a picture somewhat like the composite drawings of a criminal began to emerge.

The man would have to be middle-to-senior-aged, preferably not as old or older than Singleton, and not younger, like the upstart professor.

His image would have to be squeaky clean, which limited the field considerably. And a good public relations man (somebody like Larry Stanton) would have to build his image overnight.

II.

His name was Charles Plympton.

"Chuck" couldn't have been a better choice. He had the distinction of having no enemies and no ideas. In a way, he was the epitome of mediocrity. And the party was soon to realize how popular mediocrity could be—hell, *they* were mostly mediocre. Here was a man that could actually be molded into a president, a little like the corporate giants practicing supply-side economics.

Plympton's past was one of democratic loyalty. He entered politics after law school and stayed there. In fact, he was the only college graduate from his small town to go to law school. No one really knew much about him, except that his name had *never* been in the news. The folks back home kept electing him because he never was in trouble, the way some of those ruthless phonies were, and he brought home the bacon. They didn't know how he voted and didn't really care—so long as the road construction projects kept bringing in government contracts and he didn't attract attention. He could represent Oakville for as long as he wanted to.

"Chuck" had, of course, attended his share of Washington parties, happy *not* to be in Oakville. But nobody remembered him. He always talked about golf and food, generally using well-worn clichés. He was a handsome fellow with a good-looking, mid-western wife. You could easily walk past him without seeing him. He was the kind of man who filled out any hostess's list. Catherine Nichols had invited him dozens of times and couldn't remember what he looked like.

All of a sudden, the Democratic Party "discovered" Charles Plympton. His nomination came out of the quarreling factions and acted as a healing balm, an adhesive power of unification. Sure, Chuck Plympton would do just fine. He was a solid party man who had plenty of experience in Washington and absolutely nothing that anyone could criticize. This was *exactly* the profile they all wanted.

And "Chuck" had another attractive attribute. He was a yes man. In fact, the first time he was approached about being their candidate, he blurted out a "Yes!" that was a little embarrassing. But they all knew that any group that supported him was bound to be repaid in kind if he graced the White House. The pork would be secure. It was a gamble well worth taking. In the long run, this had more to do with his nomination than anything else. Dollar signs began to register in all their eyes. By the time they were ready to vote, some of them had even banded together, hoping to get a bigger piece of the pie if they won.

"Chuck" was nominated on the seventh ballot—almost unanimously.

III.

The Republican Party Convention was more like a birthday party. Except for a precious few dissident elements—and even they were quickly muted—the Grand Ole' Party was dancing a collective jig. The Democrats were so hopelessly lost after the scandal, and this new fellow was such a country bumpkin, that the nation would have no difficulty agreeing with them in November. "Singleton" rhymed with "Single One"—and a number of media spots started chanting the jingle.

It was such a ball that they almost forgot to establish a platform. But this was an insignificant matter, under the circumstances. Jack and Howard Carlyle and some of the other well-known Congress buffs put their heads together and spun out a program that was sure to satisfy the masses. They even bent a little bit further to the left than in previous years.

As the convention continued to revel in anxious anticipation of good things to come, the news media looked on with interest. Many of the reporters who had followed politics for years wrote about the boring nature of this year's gathering. So they started turning toward the innovation of Franklin's burgeoning popularity. What, they asked, were the Republicans going to do about the growing Independent wave? How could these new and untested voters be drawn to the GOP? Weren't the delegates celebrating a little too soon?

The Franklin-Jones tandem was getting more and more press. There was no doubt about it. A ground swell of civic awareness was in the making.

As the two conventions closed, the two major parties were painfully aware that the press was not giving either one nearly as much free publicity as it had in the past. Try as they might, they couldn't get their minds around the situation. It wasn't a conspiracy, just a plain fact of life that the game was changing, shifting to something with which they had little or no experience. The traditional stump of the two-party system was crumbling right out from under their feet, used and out of date. A somber realization was creeping through the ranks—that the United States was growing up. High school bands, cheerleaders in skimpy outfits, and slogan buttons would no longer sway the minds of the body politic. Dignified confrontation of the issues affecting people's lives would. The grand era of worldwide economic and political domination was over, and now they had to deal with problems spinning out of control—from neglect.

One reporter put it very aptly when he commented, "The Republican and Democratic conventions this year remind me of a college reunion where older people pretend they are young again, knowing full well that their unabashed adoration of the past is a futile and meaningless escape from reality."

CHAPTER 8

U rban Watkins was sitting behind his desk worrying about the latest dilemma in his brilliant career in university administration. The board of trustees and the president had delivered a communication to the dean that morning instructing him to place Professor Franklin on academic leave for the coming school year. Academic leave! Since it seemed possible, though highly improbable, at this point that Franklin might succeed in his bid for the highest office in the land, the university thought it judicious not to have him start classes in the fall. The dean did not have much leeway. Franklin wanted, amazingly, to keep teaching, but he would accept being replaced by one of his junior colleagues for fall semester.

No one on the top of the university pyramid had ever had this kind of a problem. There had been a few professors who had gone off to bigger and better things, or even to Washington as appointees to government positions, but a minority of them had stayed in the classroom at the same time. This was different, and they did not know exactly how to handle it. On the one hand, the man was bringing quite a bit of positive attention to the university. On the other, maintaining the integrity of the educational offerings was paramount.

There was a ruthless irony in the situation. If Urban decided to place Franklin on academic leave, then he would be taking away the meager salary of a person who had no other source of income, at least not to Urban's knowledge. Crazy! Watkins liked him. They had developed a solid rapport since their little talk at the Faculty Club, and he didn't want to add any difficulties to a campaign that he imagined was excessively burdensome already. Hell, he was proud of the fact that the university had a man like that around. The only thing he couldn't figure out was how this particular professor had acted. Maybe the chair of the Political Science Department could help him out on that one.

Something had to be done.

"Miss Blackburn, could you get Professor Franklin on the phone, please?" The dean had just made his decision. He would put him on a sabbatical with full pay for the semester.

"Yes, sir." The secretary seemed to enjoy her menial task.

"Franklin? This is Urban Watkins."

"Dean Watkins, how are you today?" Respectful and friendly. Sort of what he expected.

"Lousy, as usual. But I have some news for you." The dean was breaking an old mold in personal conduct. "Well, we have protocols and expectations and concerns, which raises the interesting question of what could happen to you next semester. But after giving this a lot of thought, I'm going to put you on sabbatical leave for the fall semester, at full pay. I don't think you have a chance in hell of winning, but who knows? In the meantime, this is something I can do to support you. I know it must be tough."

"That's incredibly kind of you, Urban. After all, my campaign is on a budget of zero, and I do have a family to feed." Franklin was truly touched. "But won't this get you into some trouble with the higher-ups?"

"It already has, but my contract gives me the authority. They'll just have to accept it." That was *really* out of character. "And you know, no matter what happens, you have already created such a stir that I'll bet you get a zillion job offers at other institutions. Who knows? Maybe I will, too."

"Tell you what, Urban; I'll see you in the White House for dinner in February. How does that sound?"

"You got it!"

As he hung up the phone, Urban looked at his watch and adjusted his glasses to focus on the date. Little more than three months to go before the election. Funny, the stupidity of it all was ringing in his mind. This man was a phenomenon. The entire structure of the university, himself included, had never been able to appreciate the man's talents fully. Now here he was, known all over the United States for simply reminding everyone to be *responsible* and focus on that instead of money. And he was doing more to improve the image of Princeton than all of them put together. And there were actually people here ready to get rid of him! Ironic and incoherent. Just downright stupid. Never in his career had he felt like this, but he knew he was doing the right thing. And after all, a motto dear to Princeton's heart had been around for a long time: *Princeton in the nation's service.*

And there was no doubt about how he was going to cast his vote in November.

II.

"Hello, Jimmy? We have established things in Dallas and Albuquerque. Support groups are ready to roll right through to November."

"Great! Keep up the good work."

The USA was gearing up for more action than they had ever seen before. This was the third call of its kind that Jimmy had received that day. Sitting in the middle of a dormitory room on the Princeton campus, he went back to typing underground letter number eight.

Since the series of articles after his original interview with the professor, Weeks had put together a veritable monument to the organizational powers of youth. He was doing his thing on a more grandiose scale than even the FBI would think possible. He had convinced his cohorts that Franklin was the man, or more precisely that Franklin's way of getting something accomplished could really be as effective as a revolution. At first, he hadn't expected much support, but he managed to put together the meeting that Franklin had requested, with representatives from all over the country.

In a small room, securely hidden in the backwash of the campus, they hashed it out for hours. They had all been through the various stages of rebellion and protest without finding anyone they thought could make the current system work. But none had seen the powerful leader now in front of them. He fielded all their questions and destroyed every negative argument thrown his way. He didn't do it as a verbal or intellectual game, just pointed out that they should use the power they already had, their untapped, *individual* power. Regional leaders came away with a whole new plan. And if it worked, the USA would emerge as a force to be reckoned with.

The general council, with Jimmy Weeks at its head, had passed a measure that would simply blow the minds of the people who thought young college students were all screwed up. For years, an unwritten law of campus comportment in America was total freedom, or almost, in the way you dressed. People who dared look down their noses at you simply didn't get it. That's why the recommendation from the council was a mindblower. *Everybody cleans up!* Pocket groups would have to set the example, but they expected a pretty large following. The idea was simple. Just look neat and well kempt—no provocation, from an apparel point of view. The gesture would be very symbolic. If Franklin could throw down the gauntlet in the face of the lethargic citizens who never voted or participated in the democratic process and elicit the kind of response he was obviously receiving, then they could exert some self-discipline in this time-honored area of youthful behavior that would draw attention and respect to what they had to say.

At first, it was a little like American students participating in their first experience overseas, like many of the students who worked summer jobs abroad or studied abroad. They were jumping into another culture with a different language and a different code of conduct. The idea was not to flaunt yourself rebelliously, thereby closing doors to communication, but to make a visual gesture that showed you wanted to trade thoughts and ideas. If that meant cutting your hair and following traditional rules of politeness and respect, fine. The main thing was to open up the lines of direct contact. And the hard-core members

JOHN C. BEDNAR

of the USA actually voted to do this. No one had ever seen college undergraduates in such large numbers do anything of the kind.

All of this was going on during the summertime, a student's sacred period for rest and relaxation—which made it all the more unbelievable and, paradoxically, unnoticed on a large scale. Even in small towns, where everyone knew everything, nothing filtered into the newspapers. That was part of the plan. Yet little signs started cropping up in out-of-the-way places: Marysville, Florida; Idabel, Oklahoma; Frankfort, Michigan; Faribault, Minnesota. Parents who had practically given up on ever seeing their children become serious young adults received the shock of their lives. Their offspring were all of a sudden so *different* in appearance! They almost looked like young executives in the workplace instead of students. And they called home more often. And they wanted to talk about *politics* at the dinner table! They were *concerned*! What was going on?

Amid the sometimes tearful family reunions and the killings of many fatted calves, these serious converts to ... *what?* ... seemed to have an agenda. For whom are you going to vote in the upcoming election, Mom and Dad? No belligerence, no fight-it-out-with-you glibness. Just calm, serious talk. You want to do something about preserving the quality of life in America? Well, so do we. And we want to think long and hard about it and set about making the system work better by getting involved *a lot more*. We don't want any more complacency. We don't want corruption and money-grubbing. We don't want hypocrisy. And we would like to think that you don't either. Is there a candidate who is going down this path? Who is the right person here on the local scene? Do we make democracy work, or don't we?

To most of the adults who had partially or wholly abdicated most of their parental responsibilities, while crying over spilled milk in the child-rearing department, this was entirely new stuff. Sure, they were used to putting up with the complications of broken families and the trials associated with stepmothers and fathers and siblings; that was common fare. But what was going on? Many parents went to bed after the first evening of this transformation with a pang of guilt gnawing away at their insides. The vast majority of their family pain had been associated with social adjustments needed when couples broke up and then created new partnerships. Basically *their* doing. And now their *children* were trying to get *them* back on track? Hope began to glimmer in many a heart. These kids were coming home to tell *them* that all was not lost and that they all had a lot of work to do to fix it.

If the truth be told, this is what most of the shocked parents had always wanted but had been too complacent or weak to work for. None of the national leaders had ever really addressed this sort of thing. If this guy Franklin—a dreamer, yeah, they had heard of him once or twice—was having this kind of effect on their kids, then maybe he was worth looking into.

III.

"Hello? Professor Franklin? Or is it Dr. Franklin?" a strange voice, like so many on the Franklin phone these days, asked.

"Either one. It doesn't make any difference to me." George wondered who was calling, always interested.

"Well, you don't know me. My name is Edward Curry. I hope I'm not bothering you at the wrong time." Sounded like someone in an older mold. Genuine.

"No, go right ahead, Mr. Curry. What can I do for you?" George didn't know whether it was the father of one of his students or someone interested in his campaign.

"Well, I'm a businessman from a small town in the Midwest, Cedar Rapids, Iowa, and my daughter and I have been talking about your candidacy all day. The reason I picked up the phone to call you is this: well, I like what you're doing. My daughter and I haven't talked like this in years. In a funny sort of way, I wanted to hear your voice and be sure that you really are running for the presidency. Both of us agree that you're the man for the job; and I've been a faithful Republican all my life. Are you going all the way?"

"You bet I am." Franklin had a mid-western accent himself.

"Then—and this is gonna sound pretty forward—what can I do to help? Is there anything I can do?"

"Mr. Curry, I'm very appreciative of your desire to help." It wasn't the first call like this that George had received, but the man's tone was so sincere and heartwarming. "It seems to me that you've already done a lot about what needs doing. As long as you and your daughter are willing to shoulder the sometimes difficult and demanding responsibilities that go along with citizenship, then you are doing enough. And I suggest that you keep talking to your daughter."

"Is it true that you won't have anything to do with money?" He sounded incredulous.

"That's right."

"Well, look, if you change your mind, or if the going gets rough, then I want you to know that you have the maximum legal contribution from me right here in Cedar Rapids anytime you need it."

"I'll never need it or ask for it, Mr. Curry. And I want us to quit thinking about that kind of money. Don't get me wrong. I appreciate the sentiment behind your offer. Tell you what—why don't you take that money and help somebody in Cedar Rapids that needs it? It'll be well spent."

"Well, it's great to hear that. I know I can find a responsible use for it here. Thanks for accepting my call. I won't take up any more of your valuable time. You've earned two sure votes in November."

"Thank you for calling, Mr. Curry. Good night." George put the phone down and sipped some coffee.

It was the first time that someone had used the word *responsible* with just the right intonation. This was a sounding board that usually brought out his personal notebook. Down deep inside, he didn't think he really would be elected, as much as he believed in what he was doing, but he always hoped that his message was being heard. Mr. Curry's short phone call proved that it was.

If the country could grow in the right direction, it would always have leaders. Real leaders were, in reality, an outgrowth of circumstances. Real leaders were reflections of a broad power base that elevated them and said "Lead!" Without that, there were no leaders, just rulers, demagogues, or whatever.

He continued to muse, daydreaming about how nice it was that Mr. Curry was talking to his daughter and that the two of them could come up with some mutual trust and understanding.

CHAPTER 9

L arry Stanton sat in his newly acquired New Jersey apartment overlooking a verdant Garden State countryside. His eyes took in
the scene and paused for a second as they focused on the George
Washington Bridge. Funny, he thought, that it was a symbol of a
political scandal. That symbolic bridge appeared on Wikipedia as a
site where the governor had allegedly *purposefully* caused traffic jams.
The architecture was marvelous, but no one seemed capable of tearing those superimposed prejudices away from the inanimate object
and sensibly appreciating its beauty, without divorcing the political
brouhaha associated with it. Just one of many interesting examples of
perspective.

Larry had been true to his commitment. Since that plane ride
east, he had put his energies into a campaign for truth and "responsibility," as Franklin would say. And he wasn't spending that much of
his own money. His unlimited calling program on his cell phone was
the same charge every month. So his constant jabbering on it didn't
cost a penny more. He spent more than half of each day calling people
all over the United States and talking to them about the professor's
ideas. And more often than not, the conversation would shift to a local
candidate for public office and how well that man or woman seemed to
reflect the overall philosophy of the campaign, if you could call it that.

As a result of his unbelievable number of contacts, Larry Stanton
was drumming up an impressive amount of support for Franklin. The

candidates for local office or future congressional hopefuls were surprisingly empathetic. Many of them were giving wholehearted aid to the cause without worrying too much about party labels. Few of them were choosing to separate themselves from their own parties—although some were becoming Independents—yet they sensed the importance of downplaying traditional politics. No new offshoot was raising its head. Rather, a meeting of the minds seemed to be creating consensus on the issues. It wasn't a new machine that would replace the old ones. It was a new attitude that was bound to foster support for the Franklin platform.

Many of his former cohorts were astounded by the change in Larry Stanton. They had always considered him as an organizational genius who played the game to the hilt. It took them a while to get used to the new man. Instead of giving them advice about how to cheat to the maximum without getting caught, here he was preaching the exact opposite. Go forward on honesty and community involvement, he was saying, and don't hesitate to face the difficult situations. It was like the student who did anything to get a good grade, he was saying. It was wrong. A grade was a letter on a piece of paper. What was important was what was behind it, how much had been learned. And when a lot of these people realized they had really flunked, they thanked him for pointing it out!

When Larry sat back and tried to analyze what he had accomplished, he had mixed feelings. At first, it seemed that he had done quite a bit, or at least that's what some of his friends were saying. Then he turned on that pressure mechanism inside of himself and blurted out a cuss word of frustration. Sure, more people than he thought were turning toward his new attitude toward politics. With the economic crisis and unemployment, it had been coming for a long time. But there were still millions of Americans who refused to wake up and use the power their democracy had given them. They, as had happened so often in the past, preferred to wait for the breaking point before acting. How could he get the word out better? How could he possibly reach the goal that Franklin had mentioned once as his idea of participation—a 90-plus percentage turnout at the polls—on a budget of zero?

Tough nut to crack. Hell, an election that solicited better than a 55 percent turnout was already doing pretty well in America. The newspapers hadn't played it up very much, but European countries, with all their warring and different political parties, managed to show 80 percent consistently. Ninety percent of the 250 million voters amounted to 225 million. If a majority of those votes in each state went to Franklin that would mean serious logistical problems. All of them would be voting by writing "George B. Franklin" on the ballot. And that meant about double the amount of time in the booths. Long lines, long hours, bottlenecks, processing difficulties, counting errors. All of a sudden, his mind was going 150 miles an hour.

Larry picked up the phone and was transferred through to the Voter Registration Bureau.

"Hello, Tom? Larry Stanton. Hey, I've been going over a problem that has just blown my mind. Are you guys going to have enough polling stations to handle the crowd in November?"

"Little optimistic, aren't you?"

"No, I'm serious, though. What happens if they want to write in?"

"One great big headache. That's what happens. You know as well as I do that we have spent years perfecting machines that will register votes. Why? To make voting easy, right? Now you come along and ask people not to use the machines. That's not nice, Larry."

"Come on, Tom. What will you need if this thing snowballs?"

"All right. I'll tell you. We'll need more money than it took to manufacture the machines. If even a small percent of the total population wants to write in a name—and judging from the Gallup Polls, your candidate has already gone past that percentage—special funds will be needed to open centers and hire people all over the United States, through the individual state governments. Incidentally, if you're interested, I've been fielding many similar inquiries."

"Looks like the citizens are waking up. Look, could you keep me up to date? This might be the biggest problem we have. I may want to file a petition for extended hours at the voting stations—and that means everywhere."

"Okay. Good luck with the sleepy old buggers sitting on the local benches. You know that's a federal and state matter … and it may get tricky. There are states where you can't even do a write-in vote. And some may still charge money for it. States like Kentucky, I think, require the court clerk for each county to have write-in capabilities at least fifteen days prior to the election. You won't have cooperation across the board. But I'll keep you posted." He rung off, leaving Larry with the impression he had just talked to another Franklin supporter.

"Miss Denton?" he called to his secretary. She had been kept on his payroll to do his bookkeeping.

"Yes?"

"Call Joe Peterson over at his law office, and tell him that I'm going to need a brief with declaratory judgment relief and injunctive relief fast-tracked to the Supreme Court on polling hours in national elections. In case of an emergency, we want to assure that everyone who is registered gets to vote. You know the people to contact."

"Yes, sir. Right away."

Franklin would support that. He didn't have to ask. But a streak of pure fear shot through Stanton as he realized that this one mechanical stumbling block could destroy everything.

II.

Jack Singleton wasn't about to get caught with his pants down a second time. This business of supplementary voting procedures was "out of the question." No new funds should go to any kind of expansion. That very morning, he had arranged to meet with congressional leaders and discuss the ridiculous ploy Franklin's supporters were trying to use. In spite of the rumblings, he said, there was no reason to expect a greater turnout at the polls this year than in any other year. In addition, everyone knew that there would be no more people at the polls than during the last election, in spite of the surge being claimed.

"What about the increase in voter registration?"

"Negligible, damn it. Look at the figures!"

The discussion quickly passed from clichés to hard facts, or so they thought, and Singleton succeeded in manipulating the chat. The government would simply be wasting more of the taxpayers' money by installing anything resembling a greater polling structure. No need for it. Enough was wasted already without doing stupid things like that, right? And besides, it was a state matter.

And if they made it to the last minute and found out they had miscalculated? Well, too bad. Those things happened. Besides, no matter what this guy Franklin or his supporters said, they knew damned well that not enough people would stay up late at night to vote to make any difference. There was no evidence to suggest that. And anyway, all those Independents were bound to screw up the Democrats that much more and polish them off forever.

After the meeting, Jack contacted some of his secret men on one of dozens of throwaway phones he used for just this purpose. He was scared and didn't want this business of write-in votes to get out of hand.

A tiny, child-size hand picked up the receiver.

"Yes?"

"No late voting. Got it? Blow up the centers if you have to, but no late voting."

The phone clicked into silence.

III.

What about a national TV debate?

Jack Singleton was opposed from the outset. He was so far ahead that it would be political folly to take any chances. Experience had proven that the underdog was always the winner in that type of public forum. Not a single boob tube debate. No way.

But the pressure was growing. Singleton was no longer way out in front. Plympton's image was getting better and better. And Franklin was a thorn in both of their sides. It became obvious that, as they moved into September, Big Jack wasn't so big after all. Besides, the whopping number of Independents made all the polls pretty fuzzy in people's minds.

Personally, Jack didn't mind the stage setting of a political debate. He loved it. His long career in country politics had sharpened his skills. He was a lawmaker from way back and a colorful committee man, particularly when the TV cameras were rolling. Nothing he liked more than to push his down-home humor, jabbing ironically with an occasional quote from Shakespeare. He reminded some of his older colleagues of the famous Senator Ervin of Watergate fame. But he was much more of a hustler.

So when it was down to the wire, Carlyle and the other underlings didn't have too much trouble convincing the old warhorse to go back onto the stage. They felt there was no way of avoiding it and believed Singleton could handle it. Their candidate needed some signs of courage and outspokenness anyway.

Bunch of ignorant pigeons, Singleton thought. If they really knew how you won an election, they'd come apart at the seams. It was a business, a gutsy business. Ruthless.

For Chuck Plympton, whose managers had decided to make so much noise about a public debate, the inner feeling was entirely different. Chuck had spent so much of *his* political life a nobody that a national TV confrontation scared the pants off him. Of course, he didn't show that and calmly approved anything the boys said. He continued to muddle through public appearances with astonishing success. But he knew by the reactions of his stomach ulcer that he was likely to blow it in front of millions of spectators. He just didn't have that kind of spirit. By himself, he was okay. In competition with others, on the same platform, he looked weak, very weak. Hopefully, the project would never get off the ground.

And what about Franklin? The way things looked, he might be included. This was the shocker that awaited Plympton's men when they were in the final stages of negotiation. Who the hell was Franklin? This was supposed to be a debate between the leading candidates.

Had they looked at the latest polls?

Franklin was neck and neck with Plympton.

The hell he was.

Look at it!

Hmmmmm. Of course, we're interested in a fair presentation to the American people. Yes, well, it that's the way it has to be, fine. Fine!

The Democrats went away bewildered. The networks were screwing it all up. But they couldn't back out now. They were the ones who had made so much of a flap about debating. Only this messed up their strategy. They had prepared all the ammunition for fighting Singleton and really thought their man Plympton could win, or at least make it a draw. Franklin: that was another story. He was too hot to handle and totally unpredictable. What's more, they didn't have any spies in his camp. Heck, he didn't have a camp. Unbelievable!

IV.

CNN broadcasting, strongly influenced by Charlie Gibson and his mini-revolution, was handling the debate. Their initial approach was a telephone call to Princeton.

"Professor Franklin? This is CNN Broadcasting. We have issued invitations to Mr. Singleton and Mr. Plympton to participate in a nationally televised debate on the major issues. We want to extend the same invitation to you. Would you be willing to appear on the same program?"

"I'd love to, but I'm afraid it's impossible unless it's geographically close."

"CNN doesn't believe in the impossible. What's the problem?"

"I've vowed not to spend any money on my campaign, and I can't receive any. So I don't see any way of getting to debates in faraway cities—unless I hitchhike." There was a goading, humorous tone to the professor's voice. But he quickly took out his notebook while talking and jotted something down.

"Don't you think you could make this one exception? CNN will pay your expenses. And we really feel there are no strings of any kind attached. Our way of looking at this is that we are rendering a public service and that your expenses fall more into the category of responsible reporting than that of campaign contributions. We do the same thing for important personalities in fields other than politics. Do every day. Would you please accept?"

George thought for a moment. In a way, it seemed absolutely ridiculous to carry his promise so far. It wasn't as though he would owe CNN anything, because they were following exactly the philosophy of reform that he himself advocated. But on the other hand, if he accepted, it would be inconsistent with a symbolic fiber in his whole campaign, a nut that everyone expected to crack.

"No, I'm sorry. If you decide to have the debate at Princeton, the only concession I will make is to participate here. Don't get me wrong. Your argument is mine, but I can't change the two most fundamental aspects of my campaign at this point."

"Is there any chance that you will reconsider?"

"No. That's final. Good night." He hung up the phone and felt he had made the right decision.

And he had.

CNN went back to the two major parties with an unbelievable announcement. The debate would be at Princeton University—in the evening on a Saturday. Too bad if the candidates had to change their schedules in order to be there. And they told both of them the reason: Franklin was part of the debate. End of report. Their job was to present the nation with an objective debate involving all the most important candidates. Franklin, whether they liked it or not, was important. He would be a part of the debate.

This news sent a chill through the spines of the giants. Up until this point, they had refused to believe in that damn professor. Nothing like that had ever happened in the United States. But it was happening before their eyes. When a major network rebuffed the Republican and Democratic parties, it meant they could do it. You didn't just say stuff like that unless you could back it up. The newsmen and the television people might change some attitudes toward commercialism. But they didn't cut their own throats. No. This was serious, dead serious. And the Plympton and Singleton men just had to wait for that now-dreaded Saturday evening.

CNN was quick to call back.

"Professor? This is CNN calling again. We've gone ahead with plans to have the debate on Saturday night, and the university has given its okay. Our man in Trenton will give you all the details in the morning."

"This Saturday night?"

"That's right. Give you enough time?"

"Of course, I'll be glad to be there."

George had a completely different look on his face when he hung up the phone this time. It gleamed with that good feeling he had had when talking to Mr. Curry. This was what it was all about. If the system was going to work, then you had to make decisions and believe in what you said. If you were wrong, you said so. If you were right, you carried through to the end of your thought.

He also thought it would be interesting to meet these other men. They didn't realize it, but he already knew more about them than did most of their colleagues. Enough to make their fears surprisingly real.

CHAPTER 10

The primary issues facing the nation were the same issues that had plagued America and all of the other advanced societies throughout the history of the planet. Modern life had added its quirks and new shades of difference, but essentially, the problems were timeless: people trying to live together. If the extraordinary wealth and power of the United States had placed it in a position of preeminence after World War II, that was only an extension of the basic problems into the world community. And Americans were not used to considering themselves as citizens of the world. Too many of them had fled from oppression. Invariably, they thought of solutions on a more limited scale. Even their press had refused or failed to inform them.

However, all of this was beginning to change. The growth and maturity that accompanied age were infusing a greater curiosity in the general public. Oh, they didn't know the intricate living problems of Togo or the inherent contradictions in South American land reform, but they were discovering a common feeling for the world around them. A few generations of traveling youngsters were partially responsible. Industrial progress and material comfort still reigned supreme, but little grains of human understanding started sifting into their lives. A philosopher might have described this phenomenon as a "world need" present in all nations. In spite of the overwhelming powers working to keep the country mediocre, a natural spark was subtly buffering the effects of machine-orientation. And on that same machine side, Twitter, Skype, and Facebook were doing their part.

As CNN prepared for the first three-way debate on national television several discussion topics reflected this newfound attitude. What, if anything, would the candidates try to do on the world scene? How could the destiny of the United States integrate itself more fully into the destinies of other nations, friend and foe alike? Would the economic policies of the new government reflect a concern for these matters? After spearheading the growth of a "global" economy and seeing it succeed beyond anyone's wildest dreams, what sort of global leader had we turned out to be? What mixture of science and the humanities fit into the hopes and aspirations the entire world? How humanitarian and global were our medical and pharmaceutical professions? And how did all of this fit our needs for national security? Franklin, as yet, had made no statements along these lines. The list went on and on in the moderator's mind. It wouldn't be easy to limit the conversation, especially with blabbermouth Singleton there.

Shortly before the broadcast, it would have been interesting to be able to visit the living rooms of America and feel the excitement, the expectation, in the air. For an hour and a half, three men would discuss the political future of the country, with each one believing he should be the next leader. That was nothing new. Debates had been part of the American way since well before the Revolutionary War. But so many of the viewers had never seen this professor from Princeton, and this added to their curiosity. If it were possible to judge from the press releases and preparatory articles in the newspapers, this debate would draw a larger audience than any professional football game ever had. Why? No one could really say. Perhaps Jimmy Weeks was more responsible than anyone. Some things were certain: travel plans had been canceled, trips postponed, evenings on the town delayed, and parties adjourned. An amazing hush prevailed as the eight o'clock program began.

II.

"Ladies and Gentlemen, this is a special political broadcast brought to you by CNN. This evening, James Singleton, Charles Plympton, and George Franklin will join us in an hour-and-a-half debate on the major issues facing the United States. Each candidate will make a brief introductory statement. Then we will ask each man to answer specific questions. Mr. Singleton, would you begin?"

The camera panned the entire group during this introduction and then zoomed in on Senator Singleton.

"Thanks. I'll try to be brief, but you'll have to excuse an old country lawyer if he's just a little long-winded. Force-a habit. I guess I'd have to say that my candidacy is based on the fundamental principles that have made America great. We all know that Democrats, Republicans—and Independents—have to work together when times are tough. We also know that the nation has been through crisis after crisis, crying for leaders at the highest level of government. My aim, indeed, the aim of the Republican Party, is to renew that leadership and show the world how great we still are. Time has come for us to take the bull by the horns: stop the economic downturn, pay much closer attention to the budget, decrease taxes, and provide employment. Thank you." The words tapered off into a rally signal for applause, oozing a confidence that mystified most of the audience.

"Mr. Plympton?"

"Thank you. Fellow Americans, the Democratic Party has risen from the ashes of a recent scandal with the same vigor and energy that mark this country's profound sense of right and wrong. It is an innate quality of our people to respond to the call in difficult times—times of strife, economic woes, and discontent. It is also a principle of our party that justice stand supreme. The Democratic Party has a long history of serving the nation. This year, as in any year to come, it will not fail to do so again. As its candidate for the presidency, I can promise all Americans a forward-looking, responsive government, capable of improving our quality of life and enhancing our future." Plympton made it through this introduction better than he expected. But a few beads of sweat were starting to moisten the back of his shirt and his armpits.

Words, just words. The public watching the tube had heard them so often, been cajoled by the clichés and the pat phrases so much over the years. They just crunched on their pretzels and digested the fare with boring looks on their faces. But when the camera focused on the professor, their eyes lit up and they swallowed expectantly. He was dressed very formally, or at least it looked like his clothes were finely tailored; and he somehow struck a more mature pose than the gentlemen seated beside him. As he began to speak, the vast audience began to listen.

"The two men who have preceded me have said everything a politician is supposed to say. They have faithfully rendered the image of a great nation. If it were not for one factor, I think we should move right into the debate. But in order to place things into perspective, I will not fail to mention it. Those beautiful words have to live. They cannot be passed off as hollow and trite ideals. The people watching this program, along with all those who are not, are the factor. And they are at fault, seriously at fault, for letting the high language of politics become trite and meaningless. I have no new words to offer, only a challenge. My candidacy is one of individual responsibility. And if you vote for me, then you must undertake the continuous and vigilant task of assuming all of your own responsibilities and maybe even taking on some new ones. Please do not vote for me if you do not intend to do that. Thank you."

The tone of the other two candidates was shattered. Even in the Whig Hall audience at Princeton, a short gasp was followed by a few seconds of silence. Singleton and Plympton were back on their heels. Direct attacks on them were easy to handle, but attacking the very bread and butter that they depended on was a game they didn't know how to play. Politicians were supposed to say all things to all people and get votes by hook or by crook. They weren't supposed to tell people the truth, particularly when it involved what looked like scolding them. That was the cardinal sin of all political sins, suggesting that any particular problem was the voter's fault! Such an insinuation was so discomforting that Chuck Plympton bit a piece of skin off of the inside of his mouth.

The moderator quickly asked the first question.

"Senator Singleton, you have announced that you will continue to support an increased budget for the Pentagon. Do you consider this priority beneficial to peace in the world?"

"Most certainly, I do. The history of the past few years has demonstrated the vital necessity for strong and modern armed forces. Our commitment to a position of strength and to democracy and freedom has helped to avoid large-scale conflicts. I firmly believe that a professional and strong military in the United States is one of the best guarantees of peace we can have."

"Mr. Plympton?"

Chuck swallowed.

"The senator is over exaggerating a little. He seems to have forgotten that there are other priorities. I'm not saying that we should weaken our national defense, but our present budget in military spending is draining the nation of resources that could be used elsewhere. And in a minute, I would like to mention some of those areas."

"Dr. Franklin?"

George was smiling.

"The existence of a professional armed force structure is economically irresponsible and is slowly destroying something even more precious—a sense of service to the nation. It is true; we must remain strong. But maybe we should redefine *strength*. We're growing weaker morally. Every American should want to serve his or her country, but very few seem so inclined. Our military structure could easily be broadened to incorporate national service. The Peace Corps and domestic programs should count as high as the military for honorable service to the nation."

They were puzzled.

"Excuse me, Dr. Franklin. Are you suggesting that the draft be reinstated with domestic programs being included and that both sexes be included in that draft?"

"Yes."

"How long a period of service would you suggest?"

"One year, preferably between high school and college or college and a career."

The look of amazement in the eyes of the other candidates was hard to dissimulate, and it carried over to the faces of the millions of people watching. They were hearing things they hardly expected to hear. This traditional idea of service to the nation hardly coincided with the now generally accepted notion that a private army was best and that government entitlement programs or private charities could handle the rest.

"That's one of the craziest notions I've ever heard." Jack Singleton was spoiling for an opportunity to quash this snotty little upstart.

"Senator Singleton?"

"Dr. Franklin, with all due respect, you amaze me. The task of training and supporting volunteer services and a widespread draft of this kind—and may I say that I have been familiar with these matters for a much longer period of time than you, sir—has, as Shakespeare would say, given you the lie. We are maintaining today a more highly efficient and highly trained professional army than we could ever maintain on a draft basis. Not only would there be little value in such short service, but the military readiness and proficiency of the armed forces would also be drastically weakened by what you propose. How are we, in these difficult economic times, supposed to pay for such a program?"

Franklin immediately fired back.

"Senator Singleton, service to the nation cannot and should not be measured in dollars and cents. You are assuming, as many people do, that such a program would necessarily be accomplished on the same pay scales as the present armed forces. That would and should not be the case. Such service would be a commitment of time, and the amount of money received for that service would be deliberately negligible. My proposal is obviously a direct challenge to the young people of America to express their sense of duty to each other, to their country, and to the world as human beings. And in any case, as I have said many times, it would have to receive the full support of the country in general. The honor and dignity you like to talk about are at the very core of such a proposal."

"Well, you'll never get a cockeyed idea like that through this or any other Congress."

The millions of parents and children watching the program were facing a quandary. Not only had this professor dared to put the blame on them for what was happening to their country; he was now pointing out that they owed more than "responsibility." They actually owed time and effort. As the ideas sunk in, it started to hurt.

"Mr. Plympton?"

"I just want to make a comment about the original question, which was how we view the United States' role in the world community." That, of course, was *not* the original question, but "Chuck" had something to say. "It seems to me that this talk about the military is misleading. But one of Dr. Franklin's points is worth discussing. If the Peace Corps started by President Kennedy had been considered the equivalent of military service, I think that many of our young people would have channeled their energies into more constructive conduct. And I would add that I think that our military has become somewhat too autonomous in the past few years, efficient as it may be."

A frown furrowed the brows of three generals watching the debate.

Plympton was supporting the professor and making Singleton look as bad as he could. This was the directive he had received from his staff. He should zap Singleton whenever he could.

"Dr. Franklin?"

"What Mr. Plympton is saying is that he thinks a military coup might be possible with an all-private army in the United States—"

"Now, wait a minute, I—"

"You might be right, Mr. Plympton, if we don't encourage

participation in public service by people who know they will only be there for a very limited period of time."

The debate was getting a little bit out of hand. It was not at all the kind of discussion most everyone expected—but the general public was showing more and more interest. Maybe *they* hadn't done enough thinking about the power of the military and the need for national service of some kind. The generation gap, the rapid evolution of society, taxes, inflation, the economic downturn—there were so many other things to blame besides *themselves*. But now that some of the "kids"—and quite a few really were—were coming back home and showing that they wanted to put things straight, the parents felt ashamed.

"I have a passion for military history and for decades have discussed history and tactical maneuvers with generals who are friends of mine," said Franklin. "From Alexander the Great's amazing feats, like the 'feign envelop' used at the Hydaspes River, from which General Schwartzkopf borrowed in one defeat of the Iraqi army in 1991, to the design and use of weapons for peacekeeping. I respect, admire, and support our military wholeheartedly. Why in the world could our young generation not do the same?" Needless to say, the mention of this knowledge left many viewers in the dark, but almost all of them were impressed.

"One thing," continued Franklin, "strikes me as typical of this game you are all playing. Mr. Singleton and Mr. Plympton dispose of millions of dollars, literally, for their campaigns. Now, we've heard criticism about government spending and space programs and a dozen other things, but what about the cash—some of which is your own tax money—used to titillate all of you with banners and slogans? Isn't that money being used to impress you on the surface in the same way? What would happen if those dollars were used elsewhere, in more beneficial areas, and we simply treated the entire American public like adults who could make up their own minds about things?"

The debate continued to keep people on the edges of their chairs. Time after time, the professor hammered away at hard solutions. Again and again, he made it clear that the people of the land would have to wake up and work hard, not so much at their jobs, but at being more human to each other. And he jolted the audience with ideas they were not accustomed to hearing. Prisoners, he said, paid a heavy price for their incarceration—time—and he would like to see a change that could reduce that price and make better people out of them. Why did the "common" criminal have to be treated so much more harshly than a rich Ponzi scheme mogul who bilked *billions* of dollars out of people? Human dignity, he repeated, was the resounding cry behind minority frustrations. And all of the talk they were doing was meaningless. Large numbers of Americans, not splinter groups of do-gooders, really had to commit themselves to *action*. He made it plain that we could do little as a nation to help the underprivileged communities of the world if we ourselves were underprivileged morally.

Franklin was the star of the debate. Singleton and Plympton could hardly get a word in edgewise and didn't manage to attract anyone's attention. And not once did he give the impression that he was vote hunting. Many even wondered vaguely whether he was a candidate or some kind of visitor on the program. One thing was sure: next to his rivals, Franklin looked like a human being—and the other two conformed to the images of either a donkey or an elephant.

III.

"That little intellectual turkey is gonna mess up the whole damn country!" Jack screamed. "We've gotta beat him and make it hurt! No more kid gloves. No more *bull*! This is one old horse that will not be put down the way that snot put me down last night!"

The smell of bourbon oozed through the air into Howie's nostrils, adding a sickly odor to the already charged and pathetic atmosphere. Old man Singleton was drunk, good and soused. Most of the time, he could hold his own against the whole lot of boozing politicians on the Hill, drink 'em under the table and talk their heads off the next morning. His proverbial liver was probably the best explanation of his political success. But tonight, the Sunday after, Jack was snorting like a bull, gulping bourbon and hopelessly out of his mind.

"That goddamn roasted wretch," he grumbled, resting his head on one hand like a drunken *Penseur* by Rodin.

"Cheeze, Howie," he sighed, using the nickname for the first time in his life. "I'd like to kill him."

Carlyle glanced up, only momentarily curious about the last garbled phrase. He had expected a severe reaction and was not at all surprised to witness the first Singleton blowout. Funny, though, that his subconscious gave such a serious ring to that verb, *kill*. In spite of the drunken stupor, Howard fleetingly thought that he really meant it.

IV.

"Larry, I want to see you in half an hour, and I want your undivided attention." Sharp and terse, those words broke the normal calm in the professor's voice as he hung up the phone.

Stanton, who had *never* heard that particular tone, thought back to the Kennedy broadcast warning the Russians about missiles in Cuba. Something awesomely important was in the air, something that couldn't be discussed over the phone. He checked his desk, verified that nothing further needed his immediate attention, and headed for the garage. In forty-five minutes, he would be in the professor's office.

When he knocked on the door, the usual "Come in" was replaced by the professor in person, who opened the door himself and directed Stanton to sit down, *locking* the door.

"Larry, up to now, this campaign has been a mildly successful play, acted out on the stage of political innovation and curiosity. We are six weeks away from the election and will probably poll a meager percentage if we're lucky."

Larry was a little discombobulated by the word *meager*, but his logical mind couldn't really argue the point.

"Surrounded by the sick, criminal, greedy, and immoral pack of thieves who have stolen democracy from this country, we are barely amusing the wolves. The time has come to carry this commitment all the way. I want to know if you're willing to do that."

Larry stared at the professor and began to realize the impact of what he was saying. A trace of blue steel was shining through the pair of normally docile eyes. A ring of total immersion punctuated each syllable.

The pause was short.

"I'll put my life on the line." And he held out his hand.

"Good. I want a series of fifty-minute national broadcasts, played simultaneously on TV and radio and the web, and a barrage of support articles in all of the papers. And all of it has to be *free*.

"A number of my former students, many of whom are successful leaders, are willing to give interviews. Here's a list of the most enthusiastic ones, with addresses, phone numbers, and e-mail addresses. The ban on that tactic is now off. Use it to the hilt." He handed over a ten-page typewritten list.

"Last and most important. I'm going to travel. Los Angeles, Seattle, Salt Lake City, Denver, Phoenix, Houston, Dallas, Oklahoma City, Chicago, St. Louis, Detroit, Cleveland, New Orleans, Atlanta, Miami, Charleston, Charlotte, Raleigh-Durham, Pittsburgh, Philadelphia, Boston, New York, Washington, and wind up back here in Princeton. The people who are going to dare to vote for me have every right to see their candidate in the flesh, along with my wife, Susan, and Brad Jones, and I want to look a lot of them in the eye. Meetings will take place in the largest arena or football stadium in each city. There will be no bands, no slogans, no pins—just sober talk. And I want multiple roving microphones so that people can make statements and ask questions that are important to them. Brad will be on the stage with me at each one of these. I have talked personally with the respective mayors, and they have all agreed to the following times and dates at their cities' expenses.

"Should anyone ask about travel expenses, campaign spending, etc., you will announce that I am staying with personal acquaintances at the following locations." He produced another list. "And the air travel will be arranged at the airport, by me, as a political hitchhiker. That may sound weird, but it is the only way that I can maintain my commitment. A different airline will be chosen for each leg of the trip, should there be more than one that offers to take us. And they will sign a statement saying that the ticket is offered in the interest of the political well-being of the United States and that absolutely no favor is expected in return. None of the companies will be notified in advance. Charlie is in charge of coverage. He already has a list of willing reporters.

"Security precautions will be nonexistent. No motorcades or anything like that. Each day, I'm going to spend as much time as I can in the streets. Charlie has a team of people who know how to keep their distance and let me talk."

He paused for a second and lapsed into a calmer but just as serious tone, looking Stanton straight in the eye.

"Larry, I'm doing this because I really do believe what I've been preaching. I'm going all the way, and I'm not pulling any punches. It's all well and good for a university professor to lecture on abstract subjects. The time has come for action and force to support the words. Get busy. We leave in three days. I fully intend to set the example for everyone."

A gesture indicated that their talk was over, and Larry quickly left the office. As he walked down the hall to the elevator, he was dazed. For him, too, they had been playing a new and fun sort of game, like mice gnawing at the toes of a giant. He had never really thought that it would go beyond an idealistic cry in the wilderness. Now it was real do or die. He gritted his teeth and drove out of the parking lot in a hurry, a mountain of work looming up in his mind. But it was work that he knew very well how to do.

CHAPTER 11

"Mrs. Nichols? This is George Franklin calling from Princeton. I wonder if I could speak with you for a minute."

Catherine Nichols was somewhat taken aback by the surprise phone call. She had never spoken directly with the man and noted that all of her senses were still saying the same things: he was for real.

"Certainly, Dr. Franklin. What can I do for you?" Catherine laughed inwardly because he had already done so much for her.

"As the campaign draws to a close, I'm going to be making an extensive trip across the nation. Washington is the next-to-last stop before Princeton. While I'm there I'd like to meet and talk with ..." And Franklin rattled off the names of the twenty most influential people (from both parties) that Catherine knew.

"Would you consider arranging for me to meet them?"

There was a pregnant pause.

"What sort of gathering did you have in mind? A party?" Catherine was still spellbound by his voice.

"Absolutely not a party. I want to have a quiet place where we can talk, dignified, where those people can receive the respect they deserve. You should make the arrangements on their terms."

"I'll do my best, and *that* will surprise you!" Catherine sparkled. "Oh, something else. You will definitely be the next president of the United States, Professor."

She was living again.

"You're very kind, Mrs. Nichols, but there is a lot of work to be done before we can prove that this country is a real democracy. We lit a few fires, but they have to burn in every citizen's heart. Guess that sounds a little trite, but it's true. I hope you're right, though—for them."

He paused and added, "Incidentally, I knew your husband and liked him very much. Good-bye."

II.

"Brad? George. Listen, I've just talked to Catherine Nichols and she's going to arrange the meeting in Washington. Can you handle being there and helping me get through to the congressional crowd?"

"If you want my honest opinion, I'd say no. But I can make a dent in the surface. You're really setting up a theatrical ending, aren't you? I never thought you'd do that."

Brad was on an even par with his running mate. They were almost twins, politically. But Jones had been softened a little and couldn't help feeling like a junior enthusiast. Franklin, like his ancient forefather, was a notch ahead in philosophy and practical observation, paradoxically. Maybe there was more to his enthusiasm than met the eye.

He frowned.

"George, something's bothering me. Are we really going to make this trip with no security precautions whatsoever? Not the slightest attention to that sort of thing?"

"Right."

"Well, look, now that I've been in Washington for a while, I think that's flat stupid. We may both be dead before we leave Seattle, and Susan will be a widow." He wasn't kidding.

"Possible, but not likely. If you examine the most modern techniques of security, you'll see that they don't protect anybody very well. It's like insuring a package that you send overseas. If something happens to it, you never get paid what it is worth. In the large majority of cases, nothing happens to it at all. The insurance companies get rich, and you don't have one ounce of additional security. No. I think we'll be a hundred times safer in the crowd. Are you really scared?"

"A little, but that doesn't mean I'm not coming. We should have a ball. Been practicing with your thumb?" He struck the pose of a hitchhiker.

The joke broke the tension and the two men continued talking about plans for the trip, agreeing on all the essential points. Each would make a short speech about the democratic goals of their platform. Then they would open up with the audience. The idea was not to lecture like professors in the classroom but to probe the minds of the people there. Not only would they answer the questions put to them, but the individuals who came to participate would have to answer some of *their* questions. It was a daring adventure into the realm of public contact, one that would require all the finesse of a professional speaker. Neither man knew what his limits were in this area, but Franklin could hold his own in any group.

Brad hung up the phone with an elated feeling of challenge. His own campaign for Congress had been a bath in public life that shocked his deepest prejudices concerning the democratic process. Here he was, charging to the pinnacle as a freshman. But he garnered strength from this strange individualist. In his lighter moods, he thought of himself as a modern jouster of windmills, a sidekick on his way through a maze of smiling onlookers, helping Don Quixote back onto his horse.

Yet the burning desire to see this country rise from the putrid ashes of its own undoing always drove him on. As the pace quickened and the dangers grew, he felt more and more sure that it was possible. And even if they didn't win, it was a lesson in civic idealism that he was sure would not be wasted.

He climbed into bed, exhausted—and thought about Catherine Nichols.

III.

"If you can't keep your distance and do it right, then forget the whole thing and join the mass of pushy little undignified reporters who pinch more bottoms than they do writing good articles!"

Gibson slammed down the phone and clenched his teeth.

Leading a professional revolution wasn't all fun and games. You had to put up with one hell of a lot of mediocre people.

"Miss Carter, would you *please* try to get Seattle? We have just twenty-four hours to see this coverage done right—and that's about four weeks short of what we need!"

Charlie was charging like a bull. The professor's announcement of a trip was the test, the supreme test. All of his accomplishments to date were Mickey Mouse next to the blow that they could now deal to sloppy, mushy, unprofessional journalism—or at least he thought so. Sure, an unaware observer would assume that he was just campaigning for the Independent. But like a bull, he saw the red cape interest groups, money, payola, and the rest that always sucked on campaigns as if they were a bunch of ripe oranges. Here was a chance to prove that the organs of public service could infuse some meaning into that word and spell it with a capital S. If a candidate for public office could get that far on no dough, then the news media could darn well recuperate some of its dignity, too.

All along the route of the professor's journey, Charlie had colleagues prepared to maintain the principles of straightforward, honest reporting. The very same men were being approached by both political parties with increasingly lucrative offers, if they would just show how ridiculous that inexperienced college professor was. After all, wasn't he just a *professor* of political science? What the hell was that? How could that possible qualify him to be president of the United States? By pointing out just how stupid that was, they would be rendering a valuable service to the country. And, of course, such a service deserved rewards.

Not all of the Young Turks of honest reporting held up under the pressure. Gibson knew of some who had already succumbed to temptation. It was disappointing but understandable—and pretty common practice. Charlie couldn't even count the number of events he had attended, all expenses paid. You couldn't win them all, he thought, and certainly not in such a hyper-materialistic society.

"Darn!" Charlie spit out his frustration and walked into the central press room. A bulletin was coming up on the screen, the text of which he already knew by heart:

> "Dr. George Franklin, phenomenal candidate in the presidential race, has changed his austere stance of campaigning at home. He will visit a number of major cities in the United States in the most original way, hitchhiking by air, meeting with interested citizens in the civic auditoriums of Boston, Houston, Los Angeles, Seattle, Salt Lake City, Denver, Phoenix, Dallas, Oklahoma City, Chicago, St. Louis, Detroit, Cleveland, New Orleans, Atlanta, Miami, Charleston, Charlotte, Raleigh-Durham, Pittsburgh, Philadelphia, New York, Washington, DC, and winding up in Princeton. A list of personal friends who will lodge the professor has been provided to the press, friends who will lodge the professor while he travels. No extravagant preparations have been made, but it is interesting to note that Democratic and Republican mayors alike have put their public buildings at the professor's disposal. No matter what the outcome, this trip will be a first in American politics."

"You bet it's a first!" Charlie muttered. "The first real leader this country's had for a long time. But just wait and see. They're not used to being human beings, those SUV-worshipping sheep." It wasn't often that he let himself go, but Charlie was nervous and worried.

He was afraid of what was going to happen on the momentous trip. In spite of his admiration for what Franklin was doing, he knew the ugliness of crowds and the immature heckling of supposedly "respectable" adults. They weren't used to being calm and poised. And there were paid hoodlums, too.

Good grief, for the last umpteen elections, they had been trained to scream and shout and wear stupid little hats and create hysteria. All of the excitement of a football game, including the violence, had become a tradition in American politics. Could they possibly change overnight? Would those depraved masses really be able to sit down and talk common sense and "responsibility" for an entire evening? No entertainment, no scintillation to whet their appetites in a fleeting moment of "togetherness"—the whole thing had the potential of being a time bomb. And Charlie knew that Singleton's crowd would not hesitate to set it off. That was why he needed people that he could count on at each stop. If the public was going to act like a bunch of irresponsible children, then the whole nation must replace that, step by step, with courageous commentators who would tell the truth.

And on top of all that, Larry was pressuring him to help set up the series of TV talks. New Jersey News 12 would go along with it, no problem. And CNN was good for a couple of shows and continued coverage. But what about Singleton and Plympton? How could the major networks give free time to one without doing the same thing for the other two? Sure, they had millions in contributions, but what kind of message would this be sending, and how would they focus on that? He had a feeling that if Franklin pulled it off, he would accomplish a major upheaval—the proportions of which were frightening.

As the last day came to a close, Charlie sat down and took stock of the events. An unknown college professor had risen from obscurity and jolted the nation with some new and exciting alternatives to the status quo. Taken for a clown at first, he had carried the argument to a more impressive level by mobilizing support in every sector of the population. Now, at the point where he could easily make a token showing and let everyone go back to being mediocre, the man was actually pushing on the accelerator. He was turning on the steam and charging the White House with an invincible weapon.

The United States had never had a dictator. This man, if he graced the steps of the presidential mansion, would be the most powerful single individual the country had ever known. His popular support would allow him to deal with the big boys as if they were infants. And the surprising thing was that his support came from a well-founded conviction that the man was interested in decentralizing all that power, in a way, giving it back to the people and slapping them in the face with the awesome burden of assuming it.

But what if he didn't? What if he turned around and actually became a modern dictator? Charlie tried to compare him to others—Caesar, Napoleon, Hitler, Mao, Franco—and none of them produced the same impression on his mind. They all used the power, nurtured it, and were eventually destroyed by it. A man who based his political success on destroying, pulverizing the very power he would obtain—heck, it would be a miracle if he made it halfway to the White House lawn.

IV.

"Dean Watkins? George Franklin here. I—"

"Yeah, I know, you want something." Urban was proud of the intimacy that had developed between him and his former headache. It was a vicarious thrill for him to see a popular professor, a late-middle-aged man, do all of the things he would like to have done himself.

"You know, Urb, you're a mind reader—up to a certain point. I want the football field on October 25 at 7:30 p.m.—"

"You want *what?*"

"You heard me."

"Oh my God! Here we go again. Do you realize—"

"Yes, I do. When I told you I wouldn't use the campus for politics, I was a man with an idea. That idea has grown into action and created a movement. I can't let myself be a rung on the university's ladder anymore. If what I represent is going to work, it has to be proven right here as well as in the rest of the country. The university stands for free speech. You know that more than anyone. And don't forget Princeton in the Nation's Service."

Urban thought for a moment that he was listening to a different man—and perhaps he was. No more polite luncheons were going to solve his little administrative problems. The time had come to recognize that the professor had gone beyond them all. It was a pill that their egos would have to swallow. His answer would have to reflect a more formal and serious tone.

"All right, George, you'll have it. Discretionary funds will cover the expenses, and an official press release will mention that the university is offering its facilities in the interest of free speech and civic responsibility, *per* its academic mission. I'll handle all of the paperwork myself and see to the preparations."

He paused for a second and added, "You're really going all the way, aren't you?"

"Yes, Urban, and I'm glad you understand."

"If you need an administrative assistant in that big, white mansion, just give me a call. I have a feeling I won't be in this office too much longer."

"Oh, I'll give you a call, all right, but it won't be to talk to you about being an administrative assistant."

V.

The stage was set for an original, one-act play that would last about four weeks. In a whirlwind of outlandishly daring bravado, this makeshift effort to raise the head of civic responsibility was actually going to produce more controversy than even the Idaho sheepherders had expected. To the experienced observers, like Wolf Blitzer, it was a comedy-tragedy. To the old politicians, it was a farce, a frightening farce. To the young generation, it was a living drama. And to many, it was a bewildering episode in the theatre of the absurd.

One fact was inescapable. For years, the central complex of millions of Americans, the habit of evaluating *everything* in terms of dollars and cents, had culminated in disorder and confusion amid a lingering recession. All of a sudden, the basic insecurity of this approach was striking home. George Franklin's success was the result of a subconscious desire *not* to be tied to money.

Had he been the president of an important corporation, he would have been laughed out of town. But he was appealing to everyone's need to find a more solid way of dealing with life. Love of money had truly become the root of all—well, almost all—evil. There was something very stupid about that. And here was a man who stood for something other than money. Bravo! Almost everyone was saying that on the inside, including more than a few who wouldn't yet admit it. But how many would really be more than curious observers?

CHAPTER 12

Fog surrounded the green landscape of Mercer County as George's car headed toward the entrance ramp onto Highway 1 toward Newark. He had packed two suitcases full of fresh shirts, clean socks, his best ties, and an extra pair of highly polished shoes. He worried casually about whether or not he would know how to keep things clean and look presentable. And with Susan and Brad along, he hoped the washers and dryers in all those host family's homes would be in good working order.

As they drove up to the terminal, it was early in the morning, but reporters and newspaper men in general don't know what the words *early* and *late* mean. The car stopped in the middle of the "Departure" area and George opened the door to get his bags. Before he could unlock the back, a flood of inquirers and chroniclers stuffed microphones under his nose. He didn't look at all bothered, calmly nodding at two or three who were crowding him too much as he placed his bags on the sidewalk.

"Which airline will you try first?"

"What happens if nobody gives you a seat?"

"How big a crowd do you expect in Boston?"

A young man, maybe a college student, offered to roll his bags, and George graciously thanked him. A large crowd of onlookers, curious to see what was happening, marched along, following the professor like a movie star.

When this swarm of ants reached the middle of the lobby, they were met by a group of uniformed employees of the airlines serving Newark. A spokesman for the group approached Dr. Franklin and held out his hand.

"Professor Franklin, my name is David Carmichael, and I'm with JetBlue." He introduced the other men and women and explained that they were there to offer the presidential hopeful seats on any one of their planes to Boston. It was up to him to choose.

While this little delegation was making its presentation, three different television cameras were zooming in on the scene. A mountain of a man, who didn't look anything like a reporter, was in the middle of the group, holding a single microphone under Carmichael's chin. And Charlie Gibson was up on the observation level, taking in the whole maneuver like a film director. Franklin's voice would be on every TV set in America, his first hitchhiking choice in every headline, but the entire procedure of how he succeeded would be expertly recorded.

"I really didn't expect this at all." George looked confused. "But I appreciate the gesture more than I can tell you. Mr. Carmichael," the man's face automatically lit up, "I'll take the seats with your airline, because I actually verified a few minutes ago that you have the most open seats available, which means that I will be less of a burden."

Carmichael was grinning from ear to ear.

The crowd, although it didn't know exactly why, applauded cheerfully and followed the new celebrity down to where he would check in his bags. Cameras were flashing, camcorders and recorders of all types were humming, and reporters were yelling. The curious travelers who didn't know what was going on thought that Hollywood must surely be in town doing something.

When he had finished giving his bags to the attendant, George beckoned to the football player with the microphone.

"I'd like to make a short statement. The genuine kindness of the offer made to me this morning is an example of what Americans are really like. Under the surface of materialism, you all want to see some human values reappear and get stronger. Thank you."

He walked down to the corridor leading to the plane and signaled that he didn't want the cameras to follow. Charlie Gibson ordered his crew to hotfoot it over a window where they would shoot the takeoff.

George Franklin struck up a conversation with an elderly lady on her way to Boston to visit her niece.

II.

The arrival at Logan International was considerably more dramatic and hectic. It was obvious that the period of innovation was over and that George, Susan, and Brad could draw a huge crowd. As he stepped off the plane, George was met by the mayor, a respected African-American leader, and a Hispanic woman on the City Council. The mayor invited the group of three to ride into town in a large stretch limousine.

"Hi, George! It's been a while. And it has really been a while since I've seen you, Susan."

"You're on, Mayor!" George laughed, "I've had enough hitchhiking for one day. You weren't a mayor back then. How does it feel?"

"Uncomfortable at times but always a challenge. Hop in. I'll take you to your friend's house."

Instead of creeping down a lane of welcoming citizens, the limo simply left the airport, unescorted, and headed for George's friends' house. That's the way he had planned it. If they really wanted to see him and talk things over, then people would show up that evening at the meeting. But the mayor and his delegation were a surprise, organized in advance by Jones. When they pulled up in front of a suburban home, it was clear that they all had a lot to talk about.

George looked at his watch and then at Brad.

"Mayor, what do you folks say to a couple of hours of plain talk?"

"We were hoping you would say that."

The group sat down in the modest living room of a small, three-bedroom suburban home and started in.

"If by some unbelievable chance you get elected, we want you to know a few things about the multicultural community in America."

"I already know a little, but please, teach me a lot more." George liked the group from that moment on.

"The ISIS business has changed some of the dynamic of urban life, at least in so far as Boston is concerned. Instead of having well-defined ethnic groups creating gangs and ghettos and what have you, we have little pockets of people who are either radical Islam or potentially so. Oh, don't get me wrong; a lot of the old problems are still around. But they were much easier to define. We were totally blindsided by the bombing at the marathon. In spite of all of our modern techniques for electronic spying, we didn't pick those kids up on the radar. And the way they recruit young people is still a big mystery to a lot of us."

Franklin nodded. "I'm pretty sure those kinds of policing problems exist all over the country, so what you say doesn't surprise me in the least. And I don't think further strides in the development of electronic surveillance are going to solve much. They might help you in the short term but don't go to the heart of the problem. Our problem is the *fiber* of our country. Our social adhesiveness, for lack of a better term, doesn't have the glue it needs to overcome what you're talking about. If we really want to solve the problem, we're going to have to make firm decisions to get along better. That's a big part of the message I'm trying to convey. And the exaggerated preoccupation we have nurtured for money, thinking that cash related to the ballot box is the answer, is just making things worse."

"George, you sound so damned *naïve* when you spout all that! Good grief, man, you've studied political science all your life. You know good and well that you can't just wave a magic wand and light a civic fire under everyone's butt. Excuse me, Susan."

"Maybe not, but take a look at history, Mr. Mayor. Cultures and civilizations are at their strongest when their core values are strong. And somebody has to lead the way, get the people thinking in the right direction. The Tea Party made a feeble attempt and started off on the wrong foot. Money has constantly been in the way. Sorry, but I'm trying to ring the bell. There's been enough of a positive reaction for me to be here. We'll see how far it succeeds."

"How can you possibly think that having your finger pointed at the public is going to work? People aren't going to vote for a guy who's crapping on them all the time!" The mayor looked over apologetically at Susan for his language.

"The numbers are starting to look like they might. We'll see."

"You have grit, George. I somehow never thought of you in this light. But I guess from a political point of view, you've already broken the record for free attention. And you haven't screwed the pooch yet. Best of luck to you, my friends!" He slid into his limo and drove away.

"So that's what you've been doing, eh?" Susan remarked. "Lighting fires under butts. And then you go and crap on them. Aren't you glad Princeton gave you tenure, Mr. Firecracker?" They retired for the night.

III.

Preparations at the Boston Convention Center appeared to be very casual. Very few guards, a token number of policemen around. The only really curious part was that the place was packed long before the meeting time of seven thirty. Also, a strange kind of atmosphere seemed to permeate the aisles. People who didn't know each other from Adam struck up conversations, all asking each other why they had come down to hear what this fellow had to say. There was a sort of bond between them that they were in the process of discovering. More than thirty thousand people showed up.

Here was the interesting thing: electronic voting machines were set up at each entrance, and each person was given a ticket with a seat assignment. Each person, no matter his or her age, was asked to make a charitable contribution for the event (not for the campaign), and then vote for one of ten top local charities on the screen. The list had been prescreened by the mayor's office as the most popular and impactful charitable organizations as voted by the citizens.

The noise level was a subject that one reporter commented on afterward: it was strangely low. Usually, in a large crowd with nothing to do, people are constantly shuffling their feet and making some kind of disturbance. Here, low voices seemed to be respecting everyone's right to speak, a little like a big crowd in a library.

No one really knew how the first one of these mass meetings was going to turn out, but there was an air of expectancy.

Finally, George, Susan, and Brad walked onto the stage and calmly took hold of the podium microphones. Respectful attention gripped the crowd.

"Let's get right to the point. It's been a long time since Americans met together like this, and it may not happen again for years—unless *you* do something about it. You and the millions who couldn't crowd in here tonight are the masters of your own destiny. You can exercise the supreme power of the society. Why haven't you done so? Why have you let us become bland sheep following a master we don't even know?

"That's what we are here to discuss. Let's get started. If you want to change, get your feelings and thoughts out on the table. If I think you're right, I'll follow through on that until I'm dead. If I think you're wrong, I'll tell you why.

"But first, I want to congratulate you. You have donated money at this event, and you have voted for your favorite charity. You have come together and you have not invested in me or my campaign, but you have invested in bettering yourselves and those around you. Folks, you have raised $537,863 today, and you have voted overwhelmingly at 81 percent that the charitable organization you favor the most to receive this money is Project Boston Food, whose mission here is to feed and nourish the sick as they battle critical illness. You are from different ethnic, cultural, and educational backgrounds, but you have witnessed what you can do when you stand together hand in hand. You have treated each other with respect and have just experienced the power of democracy at the local level. I understand the director of Project Boston Food just received a surprise call from us and is on his way to accept your gracious donation and to personally thank you from the bottom of his heart."

There was a short pause. This was an inverted bell curve similar to what one would see with rich politicians: a political speech, where money was raised, and not one penny went to the candidate, but with a different twist. There was no devious ploy to play political trickery. The attendees voted as to where the money they tendered should go in their local community. Heaven forbid! The media representatives soon started turning on their cameras and relaying messages to their stations. This was definitely unique and exciting.

"Mr. Franklin?" A hand was raised not far from the podium and an attendant rushed over with a microphone.

"We're sick an' tired of politicians in Washington and here in Boston an' in raising taxes, makin' wars, and lettin' rich people get richer. What we want is a person who'll do something about *us*. Whaddu ya say?"

"What's your name?"

"Sean Smith."

"Sean, let's stop wars and needless spending. I'm with you. But would you be willing to pay more taxes for better education and health care? Would you pay some time and effort in your community to make local government work? Will you stand behind an idea if you think it's right?"

"Hell yes!"

"Then I think we're on the right track."

Because of the amazing variety present, Franklin changed his way of speaking with almost every question, and it surprised his friends. He would let his grammar slip a little, modify his intonation, gesture with his hands, fold his arms, smile, frown. One thing came through clearly: he wanted to communicate. At every turn in the conversation, he hammered away at what the *people* could do, if they set their minds to it. The message kept them interested.

It was evident that all the people who spoke were concerned about aspects of their own lives. Sean Smith was typical. Instead of really being worried about anybody else, it was Sean who felt cheated or wronged in some way. When they saw, however, that their own problems could have a better chance of being solved if they started helping each other, an unusual metamorphosis filled the air.

Franklin was accomplishing the impossible.

IV.

The meeting didn't last an hour and a half; it continued until midnight. When Franklin was tired, Brad took over and fired away to the crowd. Somebody thought to bring a pitcher of water, and they gulped it between statements. For some reason, the refreshment stands weren't open, hence a continuous flow to the water fountains.

For anyone who might be familiar with the student uprisings in France in the upheavals of May 1968, the atmosphere was essentially the same. Complete strangers were talking to each other like close friends. A lot of far-out political ideas were emanating from people who never dared to talk about that sort of thing for fear that their own group would ostracize them.

They were all solving world problems—together.

When a particularly attractive idea boomed through the microphone, applause burst. One man said they should close down prisons and forget about them—or turn them into hotels. People laughed and cried. Tempers, amazingly, were not short. It was a releasing of pent-up tensions.

Toward the end of the evening (although no one really knew when they would quit, no limits having been announced), one man grabbed a microphone and said, "Mr. Franklin, how can we put you two in office?"

A cheer issued forth, followed by complete calm and silence.

George replied with a gesture that was to become his trademark for the rest of the campaign. He took his pen out of his pocket and held it out in the air. With a flick of the wrist, he wrote an invisible name on an invisible ballot sheet. He wasn't smiling. He was dead serious.

V.

In the back of the enormous auditorium, so far away that the speakers looked like ants, a small figure was standing up on his chair. He wasn't bothering anyone behind him. There was nothing but a wall. The excited people on either side took little notice of him. He raised a pair of binoculars to his eyes, as if he were taking aim with a double-barreled shotgun, one arm underneath. Through the lens, he adjusted the focus until Franklin's head was the size of an apple.

The gold pen George was holding in his hands glittered in the strong electric light and was reflected in the eyeballs of the little person.

The crowd, understanding the symbolic victory sign, began to disperse, writing on the air and smiling at each other as they left.

CHAPTER 13

"Forget Plympton; we concentrate on Frankass."

Jack flipped the throwaway cell phone shut, put it in his pocket, and waited for Howie to waddle through the doorway. The person he had just talked to was his most powerful ace in the hole, but he had to deal with his campaign manager—and fast.

"What's up, Jack?" Carlyle sounded like Groucho Marx.

"Sit down and listen, Howard. We've got problems."

Howard dropped into a lush easy chair and tried to bend over and tie his untied shoelace. The bald spot on the top of his head irritated Singleton more than anything else.

"Franklin is creating havoc, pure, unadulterated havoc. He's on his way to a split in both parties. And if we don't do something about it now, we're going to have a hard time winning this campaign. I want you to redouble your efforts in every city left on his agenda and arrange for personal appearances—and tons of coverage. Get off your ass, Howie! Got it?"

"That's easier said than done, Jack. I can take care of paid announcements with no sweat. We've got a team working on it right now. But the coverage is harder than it used to be. I don't know what it is, but they aren't as interested in cash as they used to be."

"Then up the price, man! We're talking about winning or losing here!"

Howard tried to tie his shoelace again.

"That means we go into debt—big debt."

Jack was furious.

"Howard, have you ever bought a home, or a car?"

"Sure, lots of them."

"Did you pay cash or use credit?"

"Used credit, of course, except for once."

"All right, well, do you think the future of this country is worth taking out a loan or two? Get on the ball!"

"Well, Jack, as you know, credit is getting a little thin these days. We've twisted all the arms we can. If we go much further, we'll have to break them. And that won't do us any good." Howard was still being defensive.

Jack threw up his arms in disgust. All of the intricate plans he had made were hinging on the stamina of this green vegetable blob. How could he make him move? What a lethargic cow patty. If his own team was going to let him down now …

He poured a couple of drinks and let the nervousness flow out of his system, leaning back in his comfortable leather chair. Howard did the same thing and found that it was easier to tie his shoes, since the footrest brought his legs up and there was a back cushion pushing his blubber forward. Howard was the kind of person who gained a lot of weight when he was under pressure.

They both relaxed and started over. A future president and his closest adviser. No reason to panic. Panic did no one any good. The machine was operating smoothly, and a surprise push had come from the Electrical Workers' Union. They thought that Plympton and Franklin would raise taxes too much. Other endorsements were coming in every day. The only real problem was getting the reporters to be a little more enthusiastic. But Plympton had the same problem. It was a mystery to everybody why the media was so pro-Franklin. Oh, they weren't all that way, but the numbers were disturbing, especially since the beginning of this crazy hitchhiking trip.

"Isn't there any way we can show that the guy is spending money on his campaign?" Jack moaned.

"Tight as nails. Not one single loophole. And God knows we've been looking."

"Wouldn't make any sense, anyway," Jack muttered. "He's done too much on nothing already."

"Wish to hell we'd thought of his approach. We'd have a lot more cash on hand."

II.

Houston was hot. That seemed like a trite thing to say. But it *was!*

Texans, basically conservative from the Alamo on, produced a crowd that was much more homogeneous than the one in Boston. With rare exceptions, they were dressed pretty much alike. And before Franklin appeared, they were already starting to make more noise. This renegade politician whose independence reminded them of Ross Perot was going to get a big Texas welcome.

When George, Susan, and Brad exited the American Airlines plane in which they had been offered business-class seats, they were met by an enthusiastic bunch of reporters. A lot of people didn't know it, but George had grown up in Dallas. So the crowd was not unusual. But they hardly expected the cowboy-looking giants who calmly elbowed themselves to the fore. For the first time since he had started campaigning, George found himself on semi–home territory, and he knew that the ritual was about to begin. If the truth be told, he was far too liberal for the old-money Texans. But a prodigal son had to be properly welcomed.

"Howdy, George! Welcome back home!"

A man in a soft white suit, cowboy hat, and boots held out his paw with one arm and removed his hat with the other.

To the more refined people in universities or on the East Coast, this looked somewhat uncouth, or maybe just falsely southern. But to George, an old feeling of social tradition was welling up inside. He wasn't a *real* Texan, having been born in Oklahoma. And there were many Okies there to remind everyone. But he had moved to

Dallas when he was *three*. And some of his best childhood friends, blood-brother-type friends, still lived there. Texas was a way of life— maybe a disappearing way of life, but just the same.

George thought back for a moment to his high school days. Loads of fun, literally. Worked on the garbage truck one summer. Ate lunch in Ma Gilmer's Café. Raised hell. Those were the days.

"Hi, Paul; it's been a long time."

There was already a tiny bit of Texas twang in his voice. George could imitate any accent, even the *patois* of southern France.

"This is quite a welcoming committee."

And it was. For a person who was campaigning against big money of any kind, he sure had attracted a lot of multimillionaires. All ten men in the group fit into that category.

Paul ("Big Paul") was a childhood friend of his from Dallas. They had met in the fourth grade. And for a number of years, they had only seen each other once in a great while. Paul had made his fortune in dentistry, oddly enough. He owned what you might call a chain of dental practices across the state, mainly specialized in orthodontics. George had always wondered about that, amazed that the man could get those huge fingers inside anyone's mouth.

"Have you straightened things out?"

George couldn't help kidding him.

"It takes years; you know that."

The two friends laughed and walked toward the curbside. Paul's big, hairy arm was around George's shoulder in perhaps the most personal public moment yet to be seen. The other men shook hands all around and made some Texas small talk, sizing up the prof from the god-awful liberal breeding ground of the east and west coasts.

The wealthy Texans, born and raised there, had a healthy respect for their fellow countryman. They, too, couldn't care less about money—for obvious reasons. *Circumstances* had elevated them to this pinnacle of philosophical understanding. Commercial real estate, high-tech electronics, data management, and, of course, oil.

George thought back to *The Lonely Crowd* and David Riesman's analysis of American society: inner-directed, tradition-directed, and other-directed. Texans, he mused, fell into the first two categories. It didn't matter whether they were rich or poor; they followed principles and a code of conduct. They had spines. There weren't made of jelly. This was the way he liked to remember the Texas of his youth. Today's Texas was nothing like that.

A waiting car drove them into Houston, where Paul and his wife had a lush apartment. George didn't care if some imaginary public relations man was tearing his hair out. He wasn't campaigning against people with money, just the treatment of the green stuff as a god. And Paul was really a close friend. It wouldn't have mattered if he had been poor or rich; his friendship was what George appreciated.

"Hot Franks, President of the United States!" Paul broke out laughing when they were alone. This was a private joke. They had both worked on a garbage truck in Dallas during the summer after their first year in college, and for some strange reason, nobody could call George by his name. They had to think up a nickname. And since it was 112 degrees in the alleys and George turned red as a beet, they decided to call him "Hot Franks." Every time they went to Ma Gilmer's Café, the old-time sanitation engineers (as they liked to refer to themselves) would say, "Give the kid some hot franks, Ma!" and laugh their heads off.

Ma Gilmer's Café was halfway between their route and the dump. That's where they *always* had lunch. Ma and her *girls* (the youngest was sixty-three) put up with about as much raw language as the garbage boys put up with raw garbage. It was a deep, sentimental attachment.

"I wonder whatever happened to Chewinabbacca," George said.

"Chewinabbacca" was a regular garbage man, not a high school graduate building muscles for the college football team like they were. They never found out what his real name was, but he left an indelible impression on the group. Nicest, strongest fellow Texan they could remember, with a wad of tobacco in his mouth from four o'clock in the morning until they said good-byes in the afternoon.

"I want us to do something for guys like him." George was suddenly very serious. Paul understood the message immediately, and the bantering playfulness left his face. From that point on, they talked about what George wanted to accomplish. Brad Jones was introduced and became an instant bosom friend. No need to say how quickly they took a shine to Susan. By late afternoon, they were ready for the evening's meeting.

III.

Needless to say, the place was packed, with 71,795 attendees. Instead of using the Toyota Center, a last-minute decision had been made to provide NRG Stadium (formerly Reliant Stadium), with its comfort and seating capacity. Again, donations were taken (whatever amount one wanted to pay, if any), and many dozens of voting machines with ten local charity options were present at each entrance, where each attendee's seating ticket was issued. Each person made a quick decision whether or not to donate, voted for a charity, and then went to his or her seat. The crowd could see what to do from their points in line, were given a list of the top ten charities long before they went through each entrance (from large placards), and knew the drill from having seen the rabid media coverage of the Boston event. The procession inward was speedy and efficient.

George and Brad found it harder to manipulate the question-and-answer method in such a large area, but they were overwhelmed by the number of people willing to give it a try. It seemed like all of Texas was there to support a new hero. Fancy western clothing mixed with tuxedoes and blue jeans. The concession stands were open, of all things. And some mystery millionaire had provided everything for *free*, including an abundance of hot franks. As far as most of the people were concerned, it was a victory rally.

Not to be outdone by Boston, the Houston crowd raised $762,413 and voted for the money to go to a charity called Neighborhood Centers, Inc. The director knew he had a 10 percent chance of being the winner. It just so happened he was in the audience with a prewritten speech thanking the people and praising Franklin. George and Brad gave the same spine-tingling message to the crowd about the power of democratic action and personal accountability.

Charlie Gibson and Larry Stanton teamed up on the coverage. They jokingly remarked that the Texas bluebonnets were all in bloom. It was uncanny. Who would have thought that this kind of politics, in *this* state, could create so much excitement? As George challenged the crowd and chastised them for sitting around and letting their lives get so out of hand, they just ate it up. Maybe it was because there were so many Baptists in the stands.

IV.

The rest of the cities on the tour continued what was now being referred to as a "rebirth." And more charities profited in each large city, as attendees voted and donated. Major newspapers in the United States and around the world were trying to scoop each other with more news about the new political idol.

At each appearance, George repeated his cry for "responsibility." Promises from above, he said, were no good. How could any one man make vast promises to everybody, when the entire system of government in the United States counted over a million individuals? It was like a successful marriage, he said—hard work for years, constant give and take. And it *wasn't* money. Did money build schools, hospitals, and factories? Create jobs? No. Human beings did those things. They also invented bombs and fought wars.

Somewhere, George had found the magic formula for communicating with the nerves of the nation, like the discovery of Chinese acupuncture by the Western world. He opened the door for the release of tensions that had been building up for generations. Unemployment, high taxes, bad education, and outrageously expensive medical care weren't unsolvable after all. Or at least that was the impression he made.

The coming of the Messiah was not without its stumbling blocks, though. In New York, the crowd was not as receptive to George's definition of liberty. Liberty, he said, was in direct proportion to the amount of restrictions one could impose upon one's self. And in big cities like New York, the number of restrictions, the intense discipline of the inhabitants, had to be about triple what it was elsewhere, just for them to survive.

"Whaduhya mean?" shouted one spectator into the microphone.

"I mean it's harder to live in a big city. If you want to stop crime, rape, violence, racial tension, and you name it, then you must obliterate the reasons for those things."

"How?" the same man said.

The answer was long and complicated. George talked for about fifteen minutes just answering that one question. He mentioned little things that didn't seem to have much to do with politics. They consumed too much paper, for one thing, and throwaway bottles. They would have to accept the concept of community housing close to work. They had to help each other a lot more than in other places, because there were so many more people who needed help. The list went on and on and didn't seem to please many of the people there.

But George wasn't trying to please people. He wanted to make them mad. For the reporters who were trying to measure his success in comparison to past candidates, New York was less of a triumph. For George, it was the most meaningful encounter so far.

All in all, the tour was a booming success. Both men arrived in Washington for the final event before Princeton, optimistic about their journey.

They were three weeks away from the election.

They were a threat.

V.

"Marty? Pearson here. Looks like we've got trouble." The phone was an emergency phone. It was a special phone. It could not be tapped. It linked Marty Paoli and General Pearson, and *only* those two.

"I know, sector three (Boston) and sector eight are down to red-line level." "Red-line level" was the military term used by the organization to indicate emergency action. It wasn't a question of receipts. It was past that point. It was a question of personnel. Nobody in the organization had ever had to use the expression, except in a drill. Red-line level had never happened before, anywhere.

Red-line level was the point at which it became impossible to discipline the officers who disciplined the men. Or more bluntly, it was the level at which large masses of consumers stopped consuming. The Franklin-Jones tour had apparently created this hypothetically possible but unexpected set of circumstances.

"We sell out, send a few of the family to jail for a while, and disappear." Pearson sounded like the Mafia man. Paoli sounded like the general.

"Emergency depots have already started to stock the valuable merchandise. With the possibility of one or two snags, we'll get everything done in two days."

This garble of unintelligible talk would have baffled anyone except an insider. The oligarchy was crumbling. The rule of the rich (not necessarily limited to the *legitimate* rich) was coming to a screeching halt. Maybe Plato had been wrong about the impossibility of a democracy surviving.

Aside from the government wealth, accumulated by people like Singleton, the other two accumulations of power (money) were the armed forces and the Mafia. Somewhat like the traditional balance of powers, the three elements needed each other, counterbalanced each other, in their intricate ruling status. Contrary to popular belief, they were all just as secret as the Mafia. Coldhearted murder was a weapon common to each one. The names for their horrible acts changed according to the situation and the "problem" being dealt with, but it all amounted to the same thing.

Many of the uninformed novices who read *The Godfather* believed that the Mafia was a romantic-type syndicate, known to the forces of law and order as a vicious threat, but one that would eventually be overthrown. What none of them realized was the Mafia was only a part of the whole. The very government they thought was out to ruin the Mafia was doing its best to keep the organization alive and healthy.

And the armed forces—actually, the select few people at the top who controlled the national defense money—were the worst drain of all on national resources—and undoubtedly the most powerful partner in the triumvirate. No one suspected the military of deliberately sucking the public of its funds in order to rule the country. No one even thought that the military ran the country. After all, Truman *had* fired MacArthur! The very idea that there might be a working relationship between the armed forces and the Mafia was too much of a mind-blower for the common citizen. And only the plight of veterans, the horrible scandal of the Veteran's Administration, was getting the media's attention.

That's why they never found out the truth about the assassination of John F. Kennedy.

In fact, the working relationship dated back further than anyone suspected. Much further. Marty Paoli and General Pearson were the products of generations of cooperation. The unknown balance of powers had been ruling in America for years. And, like the supposed impossibility of another Depression, as long as they worked together, the three elements firmly believed that their arrangement was impregnable, as solid as the Constitution of the United States.

They hadn't counted on George Franklin and Brad Jones upsetting the apple cart. Especially Franklin. They had not counted on anyone having enough influence to sway the masses. Ralph Nader, for example, had always been a private joke among them. They even fed some money into his organization so that he would keep attracting attention. But Franklin didn't have an organization. He opened his mouth and thirty million people listened. He talked about the only loophole in their secure plan: people. People, to them, had become robots who always obeyed commands, incapable of resistance to fear and greed.

"What do we do about Franklin and Jones?" Paoli sounded almost uninterested, blasé. He was convinced that their interests, like the stock market, were only going through a mild recession.

"Death is out of the question for right now. I'll get back to you with a possible solution."

CHAPTER 14

The Robert F. Kennedy Memorial Stadium in Washington, DC, was smaller, as venues go, and couldn't come close to holding the number of people who turned out to see that last personal appearance of George, Susan, and Brad before they went back to Princeton. A line had formed early that morning, and by noon, the crowd was double the number of seats. A crisp autumn breeze had whetted their appetites, and many were picnicking and tailgating on the spot.

The party arrived at Dulles International Airport on a Delta flight at 11:43 a.m.

Catherine Nichols was at the airport, along with scores of reporters. She was dressed in a blue suit, anti-autumn, and had decided to drive them to their destinations in a car bigger than her Volkswagen. It seemed more appropriate. She was more than a little anxious to see Brad, who had miraculously found the time to call her at every stop. And she was deliriously curious to meet George Franklin in the flesh.

Scores of people were mulling around, waiting for those ungainly motorized people-moving pods to bring in the passengers. From a distance, they looked like something that should have been sent to the moon, or machines taken from *Star Wars*. And they moved at what seemed like a snail's pace. Inside, amid children holding onto their parents and tired business people slouched in their seats, there were a few relatively unknown members of Congress, coming back to the Capitol. They had been pleasantly surprised when George recognized all of them and introduced himself, calling each one by his or her name. Brad was amazed. The man must have spent hours in front of his computer looking at congressional websites.

Among the wives and grandmothers and reporters and friends (*he has* so many *of those*, Brad mused), a small, thin wisp of a figure meshed into the crowd. He looked as though he might be somebody's ~~kid~~, waiting for Daddy to get off the plane. He was even eating a candy bar. But he was stockier than most kids.

Lights flashed and cameras and camcorders rolled as the pair emerged from the secure area. Someone cheered. Most of the people there hadn't known that Franklin was on the plane, but the public exposure he had already received quickly let them recognize him. A few went over and held out their hands. George responded with all the dignity of his person. He chatted with them all and left Brad to join his future wife.

"Hello, Catherine, my dear. Well, we made it this far." In the back of his mind, Brad was still worried about security measures.

"You look like you're ready for a tennis match!" Catherine purred, kissing his cheek (a couple of reporters snapped photos of this exchange, which would later become famous). They managed to draw away from the excitement and exchange a few words. Catherine knew that her part in this fantastic adventure was just beginning, and she wanted to take a last, deep breath before plunging into the drama. As they looked, she finally saw the professor in action.

George was doing what he had done at every airport on the trip. He was absolutely at ease and talking earnestly with a couple of the bystanders. Anyone who has ever seen a celebrity bask in the attention of the crowd would have been pleasantly surprised by George Franklin. He didn't smile and say nice things. He didn't look like he was in a hurry and anxious to brush them off with a kind word or two. And he didn't tear himself away. He made the airport lobby into a living room. The people who were talking to him really felt like they were the center of his attention—and they were. His deep-blue eyes penetrated their skulls, and he really *listened* to what they had to say. This natural ability to ignore the clock, stop what he was doing, and exchange information with any group, on their level, was at the core of his success.

By and by, the people realized that they had to leave and excused themselves. And the reporters had already learned that the best thing to do was stick their microphones under his nose and shut up. That sort of candid information gathering made better copy anyway.

After about twenty minutes, the throng dispersed and George ambled over to meet Catherine Nichols. He didn't look like a celebrity, not at all. But he was handsome and forthright. His cologne was inviting, crisp and clean, with a hint of lavender from Southern France. Catherine accepted his outstretched hand with her warmest smile. He had memories of her late husband; how had George *known* him? Franklin's comment flashed through her conscience, whetted her appetite to know the man, and filled an emotional void. George presented himself to Catherine as a natural, paternal figure. "You are prettier in person than the ambassador described," George said firmly, holding her hand with both of his. He softly released the grip while looking directly in her eyes the entire time.

Studies have shown there are four senses that impact how humans input communications to their memory banks when they first meet a person. These are based on the type of mind (or "learner") one is encountering for the first time: *visual* (in the first three seconds of an encounter, we extrapolate personality traits from the person we meet, including socioeconomic, educational, financial, and otherwise); *auditory* (certain folks remember a matter better upon hearing about rather than reading it); *kinesthetic* (some associate with memory having touched something); and *olfactory* (studies have shown that the sense of smell is most closely associated with memory), or combinations thereof. In that brief initial five-second encounter with Catherine Nichols, George Franklin accomplished a permanent bond through a symphony of those four sensory memory triggers. A groundswell of emotion built up inside Catherine.

"Mrs. Nichols, I've been waiting a long time to finally meet you," George continued.

"Well, I think we've come to know each other pretty well over the past two weeks, far apart as we have been." At least, she felt that way. Ever since his telephone call, her imagination had produced the exact impression of the man in front of her. She swallowed and suppressed a tear from falling.

"What do you say to lunch at my place?" Brad suggested, sensing Catherine's fragility in that moment

"No. I'd prefer the little lunch counter you talk about all the time."

Brad had often mentioned the inexpensive place where he usually ate lunch in Washington. He claimed that it was one of the few spots where you could meet the *people* of Washington, DC, not the horde of foreigners or the many displaced Americans (either elected or hired by elected officials) who came and went.

So it was off to Barney's Café, a block from Brad's apartment, in Catherine's car. The final "take" on one of Charlie Gibson's cameras showed them in a lively discussion as they disappeared from the airport's parking lot. It was yet another "first" for the American public, a public more and more pleased and no longer surprised by the image this man was projecting.

II.

Barney's Café was a typical, half-clean, half-everything little lunch deli in downtown Washington. Since almost everyone who ate there was a real Washingtonian, the place had not yet become a "spot." Important or well-known figures in the public eye didn't go there on a regular basis. Washington is, after all, a city like other cities, where normal business goes on every day, right next to the grinding of the huge government machinery.

"Barney" was a heavyset, jovial African-American in his mid-forties who served a decent lunch at a normal city dweller's price: cheap. As well as he could remember, Brad Jones was the only "fed" who graced the slick, red plastic booths and stools of his establishment.

Barney was not particularly happy to see George Franklin, Brad

Jones, and Catherine Nichols plop down in front of him. But he couldn't help being curious about George—and he was a talker.

"What'll it be, Mr. President?" he asked, holding out his burly hand.

"One of your famous DC sandwiches, if you have one. I'd like to get the flavor of the city." With that simple comeback, George unlocked the door to communication with Barney.

Barney smiled and opened up.

"Guess I'll have to talk yer head off while you munch on a toasted cheese." Barney didn't bother to ask Brad and Catherine what they wanted. He already knew.

When he had finished serving other customers, he arrived with their food and leaned against the back side of the counter.

"You *really* want to know about Washington?" he probed.

"Yup." George bit into his sandwich.

"Washington is the most superficial city in the world. It *breathes* insecurity. The smallest third secretary to the Commission on Public Libraries thinks he or she is somehow responsible for the world's equilibrium. It's disgusting."

He paused.

"You ever been to LA?"

"It was a big part of our trip."

"Ever *do* anything in LA?"

"Like what?" George was automatically assimilating Barney's speech patterns.

"Like *anything*! All of the people in that whole town think they're actors. Drives you crazy." Barney instinctively felt that his natural diction (a sort of modified or softened New Jersey twang) was the best to use, even if the man in front of him was going to be president of the United States.

"Uh-huh."

"Well, Washington is like that, only worse. If you wanna get to know the *people* here, you got to stay away from the feds. Once you start hangin' around with those guys, their superficiality starts to rub off on you and you get to be just as insecure as they are. Brad here is the only *normal* one of the bunch I've ever seen. Hell, we've got lots of people in this town who just go about their daily business. Normal-like. Doctors, lawyers, businesspeople, salespeople, construction workers, electricians, plumbers, fast-food employees, you name it. The feds and the foreigners come and go, mostly on a short-term basis, but there happens to be a hard core of *real* Washingtonians. If you ever get into the White House, you'll be lucky to say hello to one during the entire time you're there."

"How about you coming to the White House and filling me in every once in a while?" Franklin asked.

"Nope. You'd have to come by here every once in a while. Better for business!" Barney wore a Louis Armstrong smile as he uttered the words.

As they drove away from the café, it somehow reminded George of that place where the garbage men ate, Ma Gilmer's Café. He looked over at Brad and smiled.

"You see what I mean? That's where Professor Higgins used to hang out. That's where you learn something about *people!*"

III.

People, many of them just like the people George had eaten next to at lunch (some of them, anyway), filed in and sat down, stood up and waited patiently for the next-to-last meeting to begin.

They didn't have to wait long, however, because George was on time. He was *always* on time. After announcing the charitable gift voted on by the crowd, he spoke.

"The reason I'm here tonight and the reason I've been in every other meeting like this one around the country is to redefine some of the terms we use in everyday life—particularly the word *democracy*. That word means responsibility, the kind that involves a lot of hard work."

The audience agreed, at least to the extent that they didn't interrupt. But many of them were waiting to ask questions and talk about solving problems, the way they had seen the pair do in action (on TV) over the past two weeks.

Finally, the universe opened up and they were given their chance.

"Dr. Franklin, just what do you propose to do in the White House to bring about these changes you're talking about?" A clear voice came through the loudspeaker system, echoing around the room.

"I propose to do very little. You—all of you—are the ones who are going to do something. You are going to lift up your heads and your voices and you are going to *take action*. And I am going to be there, talking to you and listening to you, every inch of the way. But *you* are the key. I know it sounds funny, but by electing me, you are electing yourselves."

Applause.

"But how are you going to talk to us and listen to us?" the same voice repeated.

"One of the things I'm going to implement is an open hotline to the White House. I plan to establish a free number that will be good for the entire world, meaning that Americans *anywhere* could call it at no charge. And every working day that I'm in the White House, an hour will be set aside, during which any American can call me and talk to me—about anything."

Another *first*. Not only did the room rock with enthusiasm, but living rooms and dens across America did too.

"And, we are going to expand town halls and our ability to vote on key matters when we discuss them. We must restructure the flow of power. The basis of power is you, the people, and it always has been. You need direct contact with the top of the pyramid, without passing through a labyrinth. But you have to understand, as well, the awesome *responsibility* of the power you have. Every time you give some of it away or let someone else take it from you, you are helping to destroy democracy."

As the crowd flowed out, numbers of them were waving their hands in the air and signing an imaginary ballot sheet with an imaginary pen.

IV.

Later that night, not in Catherine Nichols' mansion, but in a meeting room that reminded Franklin of Barney's Café, a group of totally unknown local leaders in Washington met to talk privately with the man they had just applauded in the auditorium. There were only ten of them.

It was all George's idea, and Brad continued to be amazed at his ability to keep talking. Brad didn't know that George was one of those strange human beings who need only three hours of sleep a night. He didn't know that George had been doing that ever since his high school days. It was just another aspect of the man that flabbergasted him.

Catherine had organized the meeting, exactly as she had promised, but she was not there. She was at another location entirely.

The leader of the group, if you could call him one, was tall and good-looking, an African-American about fifty years old with dignity and poise in his eyes. The whole room was quiet as he spoke.

"We respect you for coming here this evening, Mr. Franklin, especially *here*, on our ground. We're really simple folk, but we've been listening to what you have to say. For the first time, we think that somebody at the top of the heap is going to give us a chance to do something. Frankly, our feeling is that none of the politicians from all over the country—the people who are running Washington the city today—gives a damn about it."

"What do you suggest?" George simply asked. He had always considered it ludicrous that the nation's capital, predominantly black, had received so much adverse publicity. There had to be a better way to make Washington, DC, into a model city. It was already beautiful.

"How are you going to convince Congress that it should relinquish that power and turn it over to you? How are you going to show your sense of responsibility?"

"We're coming out of the woodwork. No violence. No demonstrations. We've organized a Washington Citizens' Day. If you think the city's clean today, just wait until tomorrow; it's spit-shine time. All I can tell you is, by the time you come to the inauguration, we will have demonstrated our desire to change and our sense of responsibility, as you put it."

He took a deep breath.

"And then we want your support."

George looked the whole group straight in the eye, one by one. He was slow and deliberate, turning his head slowly around the room to pierce each brain in front of him.

"You have it. One hundred percent."

CHAPTER 15

The unthinkable, the impossible, the thing that just never happened, began to look like the next week's newspaper headlines. Incredibly, Franklin was creeping up in the polls and posing a major threat.

Endorsements of Franklin were flooding in from everywhere. The AFL–CIO had convened a special get-together in order to reevaluate its stand for Plympton. In one of his recent television broadcasts, Plympton had actually come through in flying colors and announced the exact opposite of what he was supposed to say. Having said yes to so many groups, he found himself in outright contradiction and wasn't politician enough to wiggle out of the corner. Union support veered toward George.

Another *first*.

And that wasn't all. Splinter groups throughout the country were making public declarations in favor of the two Independents— Women's Lib and the National Bakers' Union were only two. Even scholarly societies were shouting, "Franklin!"

The New York Times was running a series of cartoons about a college professor who did everything Franklin did. It was the antithesis of Charlie Brown, the inveterate loser. Big corporations like Proctor and Gamble were forced to concede that their massive power, when confronted with the will of the people, particularly when they stopped buying their products, were helpless. The hero of the cartoons never seemed to do anything himself except talk about "responsibility." In that day's issue, three of the giants had been obliged to clean up the Great Lakes if they wanted to stay in business.

"George," Larry said, with an incredulous look on his face, "you've done the impossible!"

"Impossible is not American," George retorted, coining the well-known French expression: "Impossible n'est pas français."

"At this rate, you'd better start thinking about your cabinet." Larry could hardly believe what he was saying.

"It's already done, Larry," said George, winking. But he quickly changed the subject.

"How are we coming on the TV programs?"

"We've got five lined up. The next-to-last one is two nights before the election, but you've only got thirty minutes instead of an hour. CNN is the only network willing to go the full hour a day before." Larry had never worked harder at anything in his life than he had in preparing the unprecedented series of shows. It was no small feat, when you considered the millions of dollars per minute spent on paid ads by the two major parties and their pressure on the networks to exclude Franklin. This generous free coverage by the media was a clear sign that the general viewing and listening public responded in masse to George's message and in a lukewarm way to the traditional dirty messages of his opponents. And somewhere, the profit motive of the networks seemed to be mutating.

"Have you talked to Urban Watkins about the meeting in Princeton?" George was referring to the finale he had planned for the night before the election, on his home turf.

"All set up. It'll be on national TV as well, obviously covering the entire New Jersey/New York area."

"Is Urban surviving out there?" George had an affectionate spot in his heart for his boss, who had gone out on such a limb to support him.

"No. They've decided to send him back to his research and teaching. Apparently, the board of trustees has come around to the idea that you might get elected, and they don't want their administrators getting so deep into politics. He's been awarded a National Science Foundation grant of I don't know how many millions, along with a new laboratory. So they are definitely not disciplining him. The guy looks seven years younger."

When they arrived on campus, George left the group and headed over to Corwin Hall. He was going to pop in on his class, unannounced, a one-time replacement of the prof who had replaced him for the semester.

II.

The scene as George walked into his classroom was a little like restrained pandemonium. No one expected that he would even show up on campus, much less attend a class. But rumors had been flying around all morning and scores of students were gathered in the hallway, on the off chance that the rumors were true. As he calmly appeared in their midst, a spontaneous cheer echoed all over the building. Hands were held out. He shook them all. They all started to scramble into the lecture hall, but George held his arms up and quieted them down. He explained that the lecture was going to include a large number of Latin terms and legalese, revolve around human intellectual evolution and laws—and that many of them may not understand. And he was not going to talk about politics. The meeting that evening would do that.

Some decided to stay anyway, out of curiosity.

George's lecture was on utilitarianism and John Stuart Mill, a nineteenth-century feminist and thinker, who developed a positive view of the universe and our place in it, and sought to expand human knowledge, while touting our freedom and well-being. Mill and his works had been the subject of George's doctoral thesis, so he could give that day's lecture without preparation. The fifty-minute expose underlined the romantic themes lacing through Mill's work, all of which were logical and sent a positive message about individual contribution to society: empiricism and the relativity of knowledge, the concept of associationism and our sensitivities, perception of material "stuff," the empowering of women, the concept of "moral sciences," and positivism. It ended with a brief description of one of Mill's public speeches, where the man had objected to censorship.

He ended by borrowing from Mill's *Brief for the Limits of the Authority of Society over the Individual*: "With a little bit of imagination, we could apply many of Mill's ideas to today's world. We are innately strong creatures."

III.

If you added up all the free time that George Franklin and Brad Jones acquired through the press and compared it to the purchased time of the other candidates, you would have a hard time believing it. George had managed to extend his coverage throughout the United States without spending *anything*. It was simply the force of his message and his own character and charisma that kept the media enthralled. They initially had thought he would come across as a clown, a "weirdo from Princeton." But he had steadfastly proven them totally wrong on that score. Over and over again, he had left his audience with a sense of awakening, a calling to a higher level of civic duty. The word *rebirth* was bandied around all the time by commentators, and not in a religious way. Whatever the spark was, it had lit a fire under the American people.

Who would have thought that a basically materialistic society, showing signs of pure decadence, would rally to a call for personal sacrifice, self-discipline, restraint, maturity, social concern, the common good; it didn't make sense. But there it was.

The sociologists were going to have field day. They already were. This wasn't the way that drastic changes in society were supposed to take place. There was supposed to be more violence and upheaval, more destruction and more fear. Where was all this good common sense coming from?

CHAPTER 16

"Where in the name of God is all this crap coming from? Huh? Howard? I want to know, and I want to know *now*!"

Needless to say, Jack Singleton was not in the best of moods. He was like a volcano erupting every few seconds. And the hot basaltic lava was headed right in Howie's direction. No consideration was given to the fact that Howie had been asked to do a job about which he knew absolutely nothing.

"How am I supposed to know?" Howie sounded just a little indignant.

"Look. I tell you to pull out all the stops, spend all the dough you need to spend. The message is that you screw this guy and put *me* in the saddle. And what the *hell* do you come up with? He gets more coverage than Clinton's blow job, and *I* look like a dried apricot that somebody stuck on the pantry shelf and forgot about."

Howard's frown communicated both curiosity and pain.

"Results, you fat slob, I want *results*!"

That's where Jack crossed the line. Howard's face rapidly changed colors, three or four times. Then he got up and started to walk out of the room. There were many things he could take in life, but there was one word that you just didn't use around him. Somewhat like the character in the French cartoon books about *Asterix* and his jolly friend *Obelix*, who had fallen in a vat of magic potion as a baby and was consequently a perpetual superman. You could call him anything, but not *fat*. Howard thought he would just rent a jet and fly to Switzerland and maybe never come back. He was coming unglued.

But at the last second, he turned around and said, "How about some lunch? I'm starved."

Jack either didn't get it or his mind was somewhere else. He said, "Naw, go on without me. I'll have a sandwich here. Too much work to do."

As Howie disappeared through the door, Jack returned to his command central, the ultra-high-tech system that allowed him to run everything from his office, which he had been trying to do all along, behind Howie's back. His speech writers had been going crazy lately because he seemed to be changing themes and ideas as frequently as he changed shirts (which was three times a day; he sweated a lot). He was glad that Howie had left the room. He wanted to use one of his throwaway phones.

"Tiny?"

"Uh-huh."

"Scratch. Princeton."

The meaning of these two words was all too obvious. Tiny, whoever he was, was supposed to liquidate Franklin at the Princeton meeting. Jack had been opposed to this solution at first, but he was too desperate and greedy and egotistical not to use the ultimate arm as a last resort. *What the hell*, he reasoned; it was in the best interests of the country. Things were falling apart. The stock market was shrinking like that dried apricot. The armed forces would go back to having draftees infiltrate its ranks. Major corporations were going under. All holy hell was breaking loose. They *had* to kill him. And what about Congress? What kind of sniveling pipsqueaks would move in there? No. Dammit. It had to be done.

He went into his private bathroom and relieved himself—for the first time in a while.

II.

In the meantime, things didn't look any brighter for the other side of the fence. Charles Plympton had to be accompanied everywhere by a babysitter. Otherwise, he was liable to open his mouth and ruin things even more. Not only did he say some of the stupidest things, but his bad grammar was now the funniest bit on *Saturday Night Live*. The now-dwindling hope was that they could just get him into office and then control him.

"I don't get it. I just don't get it." Chuck gazed out the window, baffled. His mind, which some compared to that of a silverback ape, was blank.

So how could anyone expect him to understand what the experts couldn't explain?

America was going wild.

And only the rest of the world seemed to know why. In Europe, Asia, the Mid-East, China, and even South America, they were calling it "growing up."

CHAPTER

I n a quiet ceremony not too far from Washington, DC, one sign of
what this change was all about was happening.

"Do you take this man to be your lawfully wedded husband, to love
and cherish from this day forth, for now and forever more?"

Only a few people were at the wedding. It would explode in the
media because of Bobby Flinders, a special friend who was clicking
away with his camera.

"Mind if I take some more?"

"Go right ahead."

Brad and Catherine knew that Bobby worked for a Washington
newspaper for a very meager salary and that it would publish a scoop-
ing headline in the next day's edition. Maybe that would give him a
boost. They were perfectly aware of the fact that their privacy would
be short-lived. And in spite of what they said about politics, they knew
that every detail about how they had decided to get married would be
pictured, thanks to Bobby, for eager consumption by a wide variety
of publications. If it helped him, all the better. In the meantime, they
had accomplished another *first*. In their minds, a marriage was a more
or less private civil ceremony. An election was a political act. They
didn't want to mix the two.

II.

"How do you feel?" asked Brad, when they were finally alone.

"Great!" She took his arm and leaned her head against his shoulder. "I never thought this would happen again."

She wanted to talk about the old feeling, about her first husband and the tragedy of Washington superficiality. For so many years, she had played the game of ignoring her own convictions, herself. Brad had changed all that, brought out the individual respect for the "self" that makes a person whole.

But she didn't. She didn't need to.

"Do you want to call George?" she asked.

"No. He'll be happy enough reading Bobby's copy and will probably send flowers or something. I want to keep these moments for us for as long as I can. Let's just stand here and be happy." That was fine with Catherine.

They decided to take a stroll in downtown Washington, heedless of any curious onlookers. The cool breeze and clear sky made the city seem clean and wholesome. Autumn colors mingled with the blue and gold of reflected sunlight. Leaves were falling from the trees in Georgetown.

"Georgetown!" Brad laughed. "It's all wrapped up in one man's name!"

Even though Brad Jones was looking forward to the possibility of being a much more important vice president than the public was used to seeing, his image was still that of an unknown quantity in the eyes of the public. And that was pretty much what vice presidents had always been: unknown quantities. Schoolchildren memorized the names of all the presidents, but never the vice presidents. The second rung of the ladder in the executive branch of government was a standby personality who always remained in the background. With rare exceptions, like Cheney or Biden, the public rarely heard anything concerning their actions. Sure, each was president of the Senate and could break tied votes there, but that didn't happen very often.

As they strolled along, Brad remembered only the ones who had

had some notoriety: Johnson, after the death of Lincoln; Truman and the atomic bomb; Agnew's scandal; and, of course, Cheney and Biden.

"You're beautiful, Catherine, just plain beautiful."

She was about to say "Thanks!" but squeezed his hand instead.

Brad knew that George Franklin, from this point on, was running the risk of assassination every moment of his life. He knew that if they really made it in the election, the danger would only increase. In a way, the few moments of bliss he was stealing from politics were like a few moments stolen from George and his idealistic crusade. He was still reeling from the impact of what he was doing. But the overall philosophical purpose associated with their campaign reinforced his serenity. They had made a little snowball and were rolling it down the mountain. Although the avalanche had not yet occurred, the ball was too big to stop. Both of them could be wiped off the face of the earth in the next thirty seconds and millions of Americans would continue the tsunami's momentum.

This reflection made Brad focus on the human beings around him, as they meandered down the street. He didn't play the politician and introduce himself, even though a few people recognized who he was and waved, but he *looked* at everyone and felt a powerful attraction to them all. They were going about their daily lives, sweeping sidewalks in front of stores, waiting for buses, hurrying past in the opposite direction, or reading the paper on a park bench. A feeling of confidence in all those people lightened his step, added to the deep satisfaction of his new life with Catherine.

"We've got to make it work, Catherine, and I think we will." Brad pulled her closer.

"We?" she teased.

"No," he smiled, "them." And he gestured toward the few people who were closest to them.

III.

Their honeymoon of a few hours together was enough for Brad and Catherine to catch a second breath and recapture the energy they would need for the last few days of the campaign. When they got back to Brad's apartment, the phone was ringing, but not like church bells (Brad had deliberately left his cell phone at home).

"Bradford Jones speaking."

"Brad? Larry Stanton. Where've you been all afternoon? I've been trying to get you for the last three hours." Larry sounded out of breath.

"I just got married."

"You *what?*"

"You heard me."

Larry quashed his excitement long enough to say, "Congratulations, I mean, best wishes to both of you." He didn't have to ask who the bride was. "Just like that?"

"Just like that. What's up?" Brad was now back in the campaign.

"You oughta know. Congress won't appropriate a penny for the expansion of voting facilities and hours—and the states don't have any extra cash for that sort of thing."

"We expected that."

"Yeah, but I've got a brief in front of the Supreme Court. It's been there for three weeks. And I think there's a chance they'll at least order longer hours. Do you know Judge Herder?"

Judge Herder was the most influential member of that august body called upon to balance out executive and congressional power. He was the only justice who knew anything about the power of the triumvirate and was likely to tip the scales in favor of Larry's brief. But Herder was a mean customer. He was hard as nails, which his clerks swore he ate for breakfast. He was well informed about almost everything that was rotten in the country and stubborn enough to wait for the right gutsy people to do something about it.

"Never met him. But I know he's tough."

"Well, now's the time. You've got two hours to put in your two cents' worth, and I don't think I need to tell you that it might mean the election."

Larry was preoccupied by the technical importance of what he was saying. He had known from the time he had the brief prepared that it could easily mean victory or defeat. In a conversation with Franklin, George had once told him that there was only one, steadfast law in the study of linguistics, namely that human beings were basically lazy. Larry had replied that the same law could be applied to American politics. With all those millions of people going to the polls, it was fantasy to think that they would put up with delays. Most of them would either pull a lever or go home without voting, he thought.

"How do I get ahold of him?"

"I just talked to him. He's waiting for you in his office."

"Okay. I'll give it a try."

Brad kissed his new bride and descended to his car. His energy was not as feverish as Larry's. Judge Herder, as far as he was concerned, could be as ornery as he pleased. Brad was a happy man.

IV.

Judge Herder's office didn't look like the typical lawyer's showcase for justice. But it did look like the inside of a captain's cabin on a schooner, vintage 1842.

And so did Judge Herder.

He donned a beard, an old man's shawl, and a gray sea cap. For public appearances, this garb was removed or hidden by his black robes, but he took a keen pleasure in affronting his interlocutors with his nonconformist look.

The picture was completed by a curved, unlit bowl pipe, upon which he sucked irreverently.

Judge Herder was from Maine, and he was damn proud of it.

"Come in, young man; just come in and sit right down, and don't waste my time." His salty accent was a put-on, but nobody in Washington dared to make fun of it.

"Guess yer in an all-fired hurry to make the Supreme Court butt its nose into politics, eh? Want us to go right in and wipe out the last vestiges of states' rights, just like we did down in Florida."

He was sucking and chewing his pipe at the same time.

"Pretty heavy stuff, pretty heavy."

"We want you to do the same thing as everybody else, Your Honor, evaluate the status of democracy in the country and do whatever your conscience dictates concerning your responsibility." Brad was neither intimidated nor cowered by the famous judge.

"Simple as that, huh? Be responsible—"

"Simple as that."

"Well, listen, young man, that's somethin' I do every damn day. I sit in this office, study the 'status' of democracy, and make decisions that are one hell of a lot more 'responsible' than yer normal, run-o'-the-mill Joe the plumber."

"Guess that makes it just a little bit harder, Herder." Brad wasn't making fun so much as he was deliberately trying to get away from the game and make his point—and show that he was not going to be cowed.

The justice laughed.

"Cocky little runt to boot, eh?"

Then his voice changed and he quit pretending to be the old man of the sea.

"I'll stop play-acting with you, Mr. Jones. The purpose of our meeting is too important for an old man's foibles. I don't think I need to tell you how important it is—that's why you're here—but I want to point out a few of the major arguments. We are being asked to deliberate and give an opinion. No suit has been filed, and no case is on the docket of this court concerning the extent to which citizens of this nation will be allowed to vote in the current presidential election. That is to say, how long the polling stations will remain open.

"Legally, and my duty binds me to that word, the Supreme Court can do absolutely nothing. If proof is forthcoming *after* the election that large numbers of voters were turned away because of inadequate facilities and short hours, and *if* a suit is filed, then maybe someday, we'll be able to do something. Do you follow me?"

Brad nodded sadly.

"Fortunately, certain precedents allow us to intervene. We're bound by the Constitution's spirit to watch over the nation's democratic health by interpreting laws, weighing both the past and the future in the balance."

The young, would-be vice president was beginning to see why Justice Herder was so influential.

"Just between you and me and the lamppost, there have been precious few occasions when we have had the guts to look at the future. The past is frightening enough. But now you come along and want us to do just that. And you are kind enough to limit the future to a few days. Just a little, tiny look ahead.

"That's a lot to ask, young man, as some of us may be dead when the next election is here. You see, we've got to think about *all* of the elections in the future. And if we do anything at all, then we're stuck with the *responsibility*."

"You all will be replaced—just like us."

"Hell yes, we will, but by whom? Not knowing the answer to that question, all of us are egotistical. Got to be that way."

He paused, and Brad looked at the bristling whiskers—well trimmed, kind of like Robert E. Lee's—and the pipe. He had never looked more serious in his life.

"I'm going to support a preempting order that, Mr. Jones, will keep those stations open. It may not pass. And even if it does, I can't promise that it will be obeyed. The Supreme Court of the United States will not stand by and let the democratic process be tampered with."

He held out his hand and smiled.

When Brad walked out of the office, the old man was humming a sea ditty, "The Whalers from Portland."

CHAPTER 18

"One of the first things I will ask you to do, if you elect me as president, is to give up your arms. I should probably say 'Lay down your arms,' but I think you know what I mean. You, through your elected representatives, may want to initiate legislation or create a regulatory body to this effect, but a spontaneous common gesture will create more goodwill than any law you can pass. That takes courage, a lot of courage, but if you really want to do something about violence, and the deep, frustrating causes of violence, then you'll just go down to your local police station and turn in every gun you possess. A gun never has been and never will be the solution to any human problem you can think of."

George was making the first of his series of television talks. He had created so much curiosity around his person that the station that had reluctantly offered to go along with the program was not regretting its decision for a minute. Millions of viewers were riveting their eyes upon that large, flat, illuminated rectangle, more excited than they had been when another American had stepped on the moon.

"What measure of responsibility do you feel for the violence and frustration that those arms create? How obvious is it to the rest of the society that you are willing to take a life? And how far does that argument go? We cannot exist or survive, especially in large cities, if we can't muster a lot more human patience than that."

He was talking common sense. Everybody knew that it was just plain, common sense. But they had been conditioned to ignore restraint and let some greater force worry about equilibrium. Restraint, after all, didn't jibe with consumption. Every other program on television shouted, *Buy! Buy! Buy!* And here was Franklin, who at the same time he wanted them to accept personal responsibility, wanted them to give the idea of possessions away, just like that. It wasn't charity, and he hadn't said a thing about changing the Constitution, but something in his message was hitting home. Every time they opened a newspaper or watched the local news, crime and violence dominated. Husbands, wives, mothers, sons, daughters, aunts and uncles, boyfriends and girlfriends, men and women, were killing each other daily. And more than nine-tenths of those deaths would never have occurred if a trigger was not available for someone to pull.

Up until now, the forces of law and order were supposed to take care of that annoying fact of life. Those nice boys they saw on TV, wiping out crime in Los Angeles, were to blame, not them.

No. That's what Franklin was saying. It was their own fault if they let dangerous weapons become household items as common as toilet paper.

"When you don't respect human life any more than that, how can you expect security to exist?"

Franklin was backing up his speech with statistics and detailed information. Not many realized how dangerous guns were, he said, because the mass media didn't show what they did. Under the hypocritical assumption that it was psychologically damaging to see gore and blood, they used words to describe everything instead of showing the real mess. And when seen up close, it was definitely a mess, one that left a much more indelible image on the brain.

"You should have a chance to see what guns do," he continued, "and then, maybe you and your children would think twice about violence. If the police forces around the country seem helpless and ineffective, it's not their fault; it's yours."

"By eliminating guns, you will automatically eliminate needless deaths. Needless death breeds fear. Life breeds hope of a solution."

George told a couple of stories about his own encounters with violence and said he didn't expect everyone to be an angel. Aggression, in one form or another, was part and parcel of them all. But if they *really* wanted to accept the challenge of improving their collective lives, the lethal weapon, the death blow, had to disappear. It was part of being civilized—and that's what his campaign was all about. They could try to solve this particular problem by any number of laws prohibiting the sale of guns, but a viable solution wouldn't exist until people quit buying them and using them.

Officers at the NRA were livid. But what could their lobbyists do? And Lord help them if some lunatic tried to assassinate the man.

II.

"You know, years ago, a friend of mine with Western Electric, a branch of the old Bell monopoly, told me about a study that reminds me of Franklin," Charlie Gibson mused.

"Apparently, somebody at Harvard decided to look into the way corporations punished their employees. The general sequence of events was a slap on the wrist by some supervisor, followed by a bigger slap from a bigger supervisor, then a day off without pay, then a few days off without pay, then walking papers. In many companies, they dispense with all of the first steps and just use the last.

"Well, these guys at Harvard suggested a whole new approach. Instead of treating workers like bad little boys and girls, they said it would be better to treat them like adults. They suggested, as the very first step, two days off *with* pay, so that they could go home and think about it, talk it over with their families, and decide whether they wanted to stay with that company. If they came back, said they wanted to stay, and then repeated the same conduct, they would be fired immediately."

"In a test case in a small company in Connecticut, absenteeism went down from 23 percent to 5 percent. My friend at Western Electric thought the proposal was worth a try and he made it all the way to a board meeting in New York with exactly the same plan.

"They listened politely. Then, some senior manager said: 'You've got one whale of an interesting proposal here, young man. Only thing wrong with it, in my opinion, is this business of two days off with pay.' My friend quit the next day."

Charlie adjusted his glasses and looked across the table at Larry Stanton.

"How many times have we said it? He treats them like adults."

Laughing at Charlie's story, Larry added, "Yeah, but will the system let him keep doing it?"

"Who knows? Maybe this movement is bigger than any system. It does have its weaknesses, you know, the system. The war in Iraq has pretty much proven that. There are cracks, man, big cracks in the power structure. As for me, I'm just glad it has gone this far. Shows we can do it."

Larry laughed again, more like a chuckle.

"Didn't know you were such a philosopher."

"Hell, I can't help it. Look at what's happened. Who could have thought that this nation of babies could grow up overnight? Somewhere behind the complacency of comfort and material wealth, those hero figures from the pioneer days have reared their heads and jelled into an idea, expressed eloquently by one man. I remember interviewing one of George's students not too long ago who was impressed by a class topic he gave on French civilization and politics. Franklin was trying to explain something called the 'D System.' It's hard to translate but winds up being the ability to make do in difficult circumstances, no matter what materials are at hand. The example he gave was the story of the taxis of the Marne in World War I."

Charlie paused and looked out the window.

"During the Battle of the Marne, the French Army apparently didn't have any way of getting troops out from Paris to defend the city. All the trains were tied up and so were the military vehicles. Some unknown French cab driver walked up and tapped the commanding general on the shoulder and suggested that he commandeer all of the taxis of Paris and rush the troops out to the front that way. Nobody else had thought of it. Saved the day."

He was starting to sound like a professor himself.

"Maybe we've reached our Battle of the Marne. Maybe people are at the point where Big Business, Big Military, Big Pollution, and Big Economic Chaos are too much. It's either sink or swim. Instead of letting themselves be crunched, people are standing up and deciding to fight it out—by using a pen to write a name on a ballot."

They talked on into the night and solved the rest of the world's problems. In between comments, they worried a little about the meeting in Princeton.

III.

"Just how much is this hoopla of a meeting going to cost, Watkins?"

"A little more than we expected at first."

Urban was trying to sit up straight in the six-inch-deep cushions of President Dickson's "victim chair," the one right in front of his executive desk. Everyone called it the "victim chair" because of the pronounced physical disadvantage it caused during any conversation. You couldn't for the life of you look rigid and sure of yourself in the damn thing.

"And you call $50,000 *a little?*"

President Dickson hated George Franklin and everything he stood for—or almost everything. As far as he was concerned, the election of George Franklin as president of the United States meant the end, the dead end of easy street for himself and every other university chancellor or president in the country. It wasn't really the $50,000 for added security measures and traffic control that bothered him. Such a piddling sum was spent in his own office for a secretary who went down to the Blue Point Grill and bought crab meat for him whenever he craved it. The girl in question, incidentally, was one of those beautiful blondes from the Hamptons. She typed seventeen and a half words per minute and didn't wear a bra.

"It's not much, considering what has to be done." Urban, having become a Franklin man, and happy with his research lab, was using up the last vestiges of administrative power at his disposal.

"Watkins, up until now, you've been one of the finest deans this university has ever seen. But I must say that for the last few weeks, your performance is a 'not pass.' I never have let politics play any role whatsoever, and God help me if I ever do, but this one takes the cake. I—"

"Excuse me, President," interrupted the outgoing dean, "I think it's about time you heard the truth. Then I can get out of here and worry about something more important."

Urban wiggled out of the "victim chair" and straightened his spine in front of the mahogany slab.

"You're a platyhelminth."

"What?"

The president didn't know what kind of look to put on his placid face, but he was pretty sure Watkins was telling him to shove it.

"Yes, a platyhelminth, and nothing more. First-year biology students can tell you what they are, in greater detail, but I'll be happy to translate. It's nothing more nor less than … a flatworm."

And with that, Urban turned on his heel and marched out of the office, closing the door gently. The president would pay the $50,000, and that was that.

Dickson, much more used to being called dirty names that were easily recognizable, pushed the button on his intercom.

"Barbara, dear, could you come in here for a minute?"

IV.

Princeton's stadium was a carbon copy of every other university football arena, an oval mass of concrete with a little swatch of green turf in the middle. But its geographical location made it unique. In spite of the sloppy mess of Nassau Street, remembered fondly by activists in years past, the city of Princeton remained a privileged chunk of real estate. Climbing the few low-lying hills around the city, the town dominated one of the most picturesque scenes. On campus, a tiger statue stared back at onlookers, unafraid, with a piercing gaze, ready to pounce.

When dusk enveloped the area, and particularly when the air was smog-fog free, sunset from the Princeton stadium was almost a happening. Psychedelic lights scintillated up one avenue of the college town, and another street jettisoned a second batch of luminosity as the stadium projected its skeleton onto the stars.

Sensitive people have a tendency to become poetic when they see something like that.

Even calloused, scornful characters like Dickson have the same tendency.

That's the way it was for the last big encounter session of George Franklin's campaign. Thousands of students, parents, teachers, and curious citizens were filing into the edifice, already more than awe-struck by the environment they lived in every day. Nassau looked as though the pied piper was summoning them to the stadium. It was a magnificent union of human, atmospheric, and geodesic factors that only God could have concocted for the occasion. The total conglomeration of such normally incongruous elements produced more basic harmony than your typical a cappella choir.

The evening was warm, Indian summer warm, and the shuffling feet of all those people echoed agreement as they changed seats four or five times, making room for new arrivals. The charitable giving system was not in place. Nobody was there to usher them to reserved places, paid for in cash. No, they just smiled at each other and looked at the first few evening lights, making friends as they jostled around.

Many of the enthusiastic newcomers to Franklin's philosophy repeated the only campaign slogan that had caught on, the imaginary signature in the air. The gesture looked like clients in a busy restaurant motioning to the waiter for the check.

All of these involuntary theatrics created the perfect scene for George's arrival. He walked out onto the field and climbed up onto the wooden platform in the middle of the fifty-yard line, amid thundering applause. He was there alone, without Brad and Susan. His mood was optimistic.

He didn't raise his hands to calm the crowd and didn't respond to the numerous hands writing his name in the air. He just turned in every direction and let the noise subside by itself.

When the last pair of clapping hands had died away into the sunset and you could hear the gentle wind blowing down through Cannon Green, he began to speak.

"We couldn't have picked a more beautiful time to talk about getting things together," he said, motioning toward the sky.

People laughed, and a few applauded again.

"This is the last public assembly on my agenda before you all go to the polls. I don't think I could really say all I'd like to, and hear everything you have to say, if we held a meeting like this every evening for a year. But I want to start off by declaring that I intend to come as close to that as possible. The power structure of this democracy is *you*, and it always has been. Maybe some of you just haven't thought about it enough. Your voices, all of them, have to be heard—while you listen respectfully to the person next to you. By helping them solve their problems, you all know that you'll come close to solving your own. And don't kid yourselves either; we have a myriad of problems to solve."

George then started spelling them out, the way he saw them. He repeated the need for education, in their institutions and in their daily lives and homes; the self-discipline necessary to address the economic crisis, sickness, poverty, discrimination; the burden of making their society more livable, more human—no matter what material comforts were at hand.

He was applauded constantly, more than at any of the other meetings, and often had to stop and wait for the noise to die down.

After twenty minutes of summarizing the basic elements of his campaign, George spoke to the majority of young people in the audience and introduced the subject that Jimmy Weeks had been waiting for: the specific responsibilities of the younger generation.

"After World War II, the surviving generations all over the world had a common psychological reaction. That war looked like it might prove the falsity of assumptions made in 1918. When were we going to see the war to end all wars? Of course, it wasn't to be. There were going to be wars, horrible wars, forever, or so it seemed. So the general trend among young people was to forget about the future and grab whatever pleasure was at hand. We tapped into the riches of the earth and constantly invented new ways to use them. And today, among other things, we are gobbling up our natural resources faster than ever. Most of you are keenly aware of that. But what are you doing to stop it? If you want to accept *your* responsibility, you've got to start thinking about your own grandchildren and their grandchildren. That's hard to do when you're young, and it's much more of a sacrifice than your parents ever dreamed it would be."

He continued elaborating his point of view, challenging every generation present in the crowd.

V.

Jimmy and his fellow students were listening to the speech and communicating with each other on a secure wireless system, like the ones you see with little earpieces on *NCIS*. They were placed in strategic areas around the stadium, every nook and cranny of which they knew by heart. In spite of their amazing intelligence work, they had received no specific details concerning the assassination attempt. All they knew was that something was supposed to happen, something catastrophic. Close to or far away from the platform, they didn't know.

Not too high up in the lower section on the fifty-yard line, a small spectator seemed to be listening as hard as the people around him. He applauded enthusiastically and was quick to silence when the loudspeaker system boomed anew. Dressed like a student in pullover, jeans, and sandals, he drew no one's attention in particular.

A closer examination, however, would have attracted the experienced eye, aside from the fact that he was obviously a dwarf. Hanging from his neck was a long pair of field glasses. They stretched from his throat to well below his abdomen and gave him the comic appearance of a child with his father's binoculars. A short leather strap kept them right under his chin. The central pivot ordinarily seen on large binoculars was hollow at one end. No one, even people close to him, could have seen this, since the apparatus was facing down. In fact, one of Jimmy's USA commandos was only a few feet away. But a well-trained security guard would have wondered why the dwarf had chosen a seat so close to the field, where he had no need for magnifying glasses. Maybe he hadn't expected to find a seat so close.

"You have in front of you, and probably until the day you die, a series of well-entrenched organisms that have attacked the balance of modern life: the Mafia, drug cartels, government agencies, CEO's of corporations, logistical giants in the armed services, prejudice, greed, and destructive egotism. They will not change by your wishing it so. The only way to combat these forces and build a meaningful life for the future is to create new traditions, new pleasures, and sacrifice the ones that have been created for you and which provide weakness instead of individual strength."

The tiny hands raised the heavy binoculars to a horizontal position as he sat on his knees, only a few inches higher than the head of the person in front of him. A rod was screwed into the bottom side of the barrel, extending down to the seat in order to keep it steady.

"I can't paint a rosy picture of the future. You all know that we have been well on our way to ruining it. And if any of you feel the slightest bit of encouragement here tonight, let me tell you that you're going to have to work at maintaining that feeling, on your own, for a long time to come, many more years than the four or eight during which a single person can hold the office of president. The force has got to come from within you."

A small pair of eyes looked into the large, round circle and began focusing, quickly, on the speaker's platform. The fuzzy image jumped into clarity and fuzzed again for a fraction of a second.

"So you see, my campaign is not a promise, a wishful dream that will satisfy all of your desires. Far from that. If you vote for me, you're in for a lot of hard work, the results of which may not be felt until long after you and I are dead ..."

The silenced shot had to be perfect, dead center on the first turn of the spring mechanism, with only three seconds for number two. Steel nerves had to control those little fingers, because even without the possibility of a ricochet attracting attention, the two *spits* of the ingenious firearm were likely to make someone curious.

"*Weeks!*" a voice screamed into Jimmy's ears. "Who's that kid? Row ten, aisle five!"

Jimmy's own glasses pivoted with a jerk and focused in.

"It's an uphill battle all the way, the rewards of which—"

"Grab him, Mark, *now!*"

Spit.

CHAPTER 19

Three seconds can be a long or a short period of time, depending on your point of view. An astronaut, for example, who is three seconds off on reentry, can say good-bye and happy sizzling. A sailboat skipper in a regatta who is three seconds over the line at the start has to go all the way back around—and is usually last.

Steel-nerved Tiny blew his three seconds, mainly because he didn't have them. Mark's athletic nerves moved faster and with a lot more adrenaline. Just as the *spit* gushed out of the end of the gun, an iron claw yanked the assassin off his knees and literally catapulted him into the air. He looked like a circus clown doing a somersault. The cyanide-poisoned second bullet (the first one having missed) disappeared into the night air and embedded itself harmlessly into the front side of a tackling dummy. Two women screamed.

George interrupted his talk and looked over at the disturbance, unaware of what had just happened. Then he saw Jimmy Weeks running out onto the field.

The entire stadium crowd was on its feet, sensing the first few moments of what might become a panic.

"What happened?" George echoed everyone's sentiments into the microphone. "This is Jimmy Weeks, editor of the *Daily Princetonian*."

"An assassination attempt has just been made on your life," blurted Jimmy, "and we have the person over there." He pointed to the sidelines.

Four policemen were galloping across the field in their uniforms, followed by the TV cameras covering the event. The noise level was now almost to the level of drowning out the microphone.

"*Listen!*" George shouted into the mike, turning up the volume at the same time.

The crowd was so used to a calmer, milder tone of voice, that the imperative command momentarily caught their attention. They fell silent.

"*Don't panic!*" he boomed again.

George was completely in control and master of the situation.

"This shouldn't come as a surprise to any of you. It's the very thing we have to change. We *must* stop thinking that death is the answer."

By this time, half of the United States was on its feet, just like the crowd. Commentators were screaming into their microphones like excited sportscasters, and the people at home were tenser than the live audience. What probably surprised all of them the most was the comportment of the candidate. Not the slightest bit of fear could be seen on his face, nor heard in his voice. He was injecting the kind of leadership into the moment that could leave no doubts about his character and strength. For the millions of people observing the scene, they had a live example of how their future president would react under pressure. There was not much doubt about what kind of a commander in chief he would make.

As the seconds ticked away and the policemen took custody of the tiny would-be killer, the cameras were intermittently shifting from the aggressor to Franklin. Two gargantuan policemen each grabbed one of the dwarf's arms and hoisted him in the air, carrying him toward a police car, his legs kicking in the air like a small child about to receive a spanking.

Nothing was very clear, since the perp was surrounded and of such small stature that only his head was occasionally visible. They began to hustle him out through the closest entryway tunnel, while the crowd remained on its feet, not yet stampeding. At this moment, the cameras all focused on the platform.

"Get down from the platform, Professor; there might be more!" someone shouted into one of the roving mikes.

"*No!*" George said, loud and clear. "One man, one senator, one congressman, or one mayor cannot and never will be totally responsible for your security. Professional police can help, but the strength, the *vital* strength in situations like this, has to come from you. *Look* at each other and search for that strength."

They did, with a menacing glare that would have put fear into the heart of any other assassin present. The huge mass of people was taking control of the situation on its own. Cool and with no sign of panic, they rose to the occasion. George's leadership held.

"Do you *see* what I mean? Do you have some kind of idea of the work that lies ahead?" George now moved to the side of the platform and calmly walked down the steps. With incredible self-control, the crowd followed his example and started filing out of the stadium. Some were walking faster than others, but there was no pushing or shoving. It was like the orderly evacuation of the US Airways plane that ditched in the Hudson under Sully's command. And the whole nation was watching.

II.

News media throughout the United States and abroad were vibrating with bits and pieces of the climactic drama. Almost everyone had expected something like this to happen. Too many other public figures had been "eliminated" when they got to the daring point of really making fundamental changes, and George Franklin had challenged the limits of their ability to change right from the beginning of his campaign. Some interest group was bound to try and kill him.

All of them had seen his grit. This was no softy in an academic ivory tower. It gave them more hope than all of the sensible words he had poured forth in the past few weeks. No matter how little experience he might have in government, this was the kind of person they could trust in high office. Parents and children, bureaucrats and businessmen now knew that Franklin was capable of following his own principles, ready to go all the way. For some, he would be too far to the left politically; for others, he would be too far to the right. But for all of them, his sincerity and sense of purpose were as solid as a rock.

III.

"We have only a few alternatives for the future: an easy, self-destructive, and egotistical attitude that is basically inhuman, or a very hard road toward security and equilibrium in the world."

George was making his final speech—a replay of it, actually—on the ten o'clock news. His sober tone reflected no more gravity than in previous speeches, but everyone listening to the program was looking for the effects of the assassination attempt. In addition, some information was already surfacing about the assassin. They were more aware of how ruthless the triumvirate could be—although a clear picture of what it really was would come later—shocked by the extremes to which groups in their own society had gone to drain them of any real say in government, and emotionally disturbed by the events. New realities, brand new, were surfacing in their conscious minds.

"Tiny" committed suicide on the way to the jail, but before he swallowed the pill, he had spilled enough of the beans for the public to hear what was going on. And the USA had made a few of its dossiers available (how did they get them?) implying that members of the Singleton camp were involved in some way.

The greedy struggle for power, usually hidden in secrecy, was laid open for the common citizen to see—in all its lurid detail. Singleton was denying everything, but it was obvious that his chances of being elected were compromised.

"Chuck" Plympton became, instantaneously, the only other candidate in the race. He was essentially nobody, but next to Singleton, he at least appeared to represent the Democratic Party honorably. Poor Chuck gave most people the impression that he would occupy the White House like a wet washcloth occupies the bathtub. Compared to Franklin, especially after the attempted assassination in Princeton, Plympton was weak.

"The severity of what I propose may be interpreted by some of you as an exaggeration, too bleak a picture of what we are up against. But I think you will see that life can be just as fulfilling, perhaps even happier, when every day brings you closer to common goals that are good for us all."

Charlie Gibson was behind the camera, focusing on America's new hero. He tried to picture the man sitting in the Oval Office of the White House and ending his announcements with the seal of the president projected onto the screen. There was an aura of dignity attached to his person that again roused memories of Jack Kennedy. But a wholly different quality emerged as he listened, one that spelled relief for the first time, relief from the hassle of underhanded tactics and the frenzy of backstabbing and dirty politics.

The hour seemed to pass by in the space of a few minutes, and even the camera crew was surprised when George made his final statement.

"When you go to the polls tomorrow, please don't let the idealistic words I've been pronouncing influence you superficially. The act you are about to perform is too important for that. Remember that I am asking *you* to commit, that electing me as your president will mean a far greater participation on *your* part, all the way down the line. We will all live up to that commitment together. Thank you."

The lights dimmed immediately, and a smaller panel showed the CNN commentator saying, "You have just heard the last ..."

Charlie walked over to George Franklin and silently held out his hand. The two men looked at each other over the heavy electric cables running like snakes across the set. Various members of the crew shook hands with him as well, convinced that he would win the election within twenty-four hours. The small group emerged on the sidewalk outside.

"Do you want us to cover your voting tomorrow? If we don't, somebody else will." Charlie didn't want a sense of finality in their adventure to settle in.

"Whatever you want to do, Charlie," George replied, a little wistfully. "What do you say to a cup of coffee?"

They walked down the brightly lit hillside and stopped in at a French café called Chez Alice, which reminded George a bit of Barney's Café in Washington. Warm and inviting. They chose a booth next to the window where they could watch the passersby. A foreign-looking waitress came up to take their order.

George took one look at her and said, "Deux cafés, s'il vous plaît, bien serrés."

Having recognized him immediately, she was somewhat taken aback by the fact that he was speaking her native language without an accent. "Tout de suite, Monsieur le Président!"

The steaming cups arrived and George seemed to relax, as though he had just started a vacation.

"You've come a long way from that first night in Princeton," Charlie commented banally.

"Pretty amazing, isn't it? But you know as well as I do that it's the people who have come a long way, not just me. All I did was show them it was possible, and look what they've done! If I'm elected tomorrow, we're in for at least four years of those kinds of possibilities." George was glowing. He looked out of the window and continued.

"You know, with this kind of spirit, we can turn it all around. Human potential is the most overwhelming thing nature has produced. The reserves of energy used up until now for historical catastrophes are unknown. If we can tap into just a small portion of them for humanity, every American will become a world leader in the true sense of the word."

As they pushed their chairs in and stood up to leave, an elderly couple nodded and smiled warmly. The husband raised his hand, bony with arthritis and shaking a little, and wrote an imaginary signature in the air.

IV.

"As in every election year, we will stay with you until it is clear that one of the candidates has won, and a running commentary on each state and congressional district will light up on the board you see behind me." Wolf Blitzer was installed behind a triangular desk for the evening presentation of returns.

"This year, in perhaps the most extraordinary circumstances of any election in American history, it may be a long night. As most of you know, the Supreme Court has issued a preempting order for polling stations to remain open late into the night, in order to permit voters for George Franklin to write in his name, a process that takes longer than electronic voting. Scanty indications from the East Coast have already shown that this measure was necessary, since thousands of voters are still lined up outside. Here is our special report."

Brad and Catherine Jones were watching the news in Brad's small apartment. They planned to go out to Catherine's mansion later in the evening for the first informal reunion of George's supporters. Jimmy Weeks, Charlie Gibson, and Larry Stanton, along with a few reporters and commentators, would be their guests. They had to pick up Charlie and Larry at the airport.

"Blitzer won't get any sleep tonight," laughed Brad. "They may not close those polls until tomorrow morning!"

"*May* not?" Catherine teased.

When they arrived at National, they were surprised to see an almost deserted terminal building. There were just the normal employees and a few travelers.

Charlie and Larry looked tired but elated as they joined the newlyweds.

"We could see those voting lines shining up all across the country!" Larry said as they put their bags in the car. "Do we celebrate a victory this evening, Mr. Vice President?"

"That's what the party's for, Larry, since we've already won, no matter what the results. It looks like you've broken every personal record in your career with this one."

The car radio, on some channel that was patching it through live, gave them Wolf Blitzer's voice again.

"Computer analyses, which are generally possible in projecting the outcome after a certain count, will be of no use in this year's election, since so many of the ballots must be counted by hand. It's almost like a pioneer election in the twenty-first century."

They drove up to the mansion and parked in front of the main entrance, next to the few cars already there. They were all inexpensive models.

In the comfortable living room, a large flat-screen TV was turned on, and a fire was blazing in the fireplace. Jimmy Weeks was waiting, dressed in a blue suit and red tie. None of them knew how important a role he had played in the campaign, but they were all impressed with his knowledge of what was going on in university towns.

He made a surprise announcement.

"We've decided to disband the USA. After tonight, it doesn't need to exist anymore."

Their talk was not the excited kind you might expect at a victory rally. It was measured and varied from the election to politics in general, to history and the future. Late in the night, when Wolf began to show signs of fatigue, it became apparent that they would be there until the wee hours of the morning. Brad opened a couple of bottles of champagne, and they cheered when a few senatorial positions went to Independents.

At one o'clock in the morning, the phone rang.

It was George. He asked to speak to Brad.

"I just want to pass something on to the whole group, and I want it to sound as undramatic as possible. Tell Catherine, Larry, Charlie, and Jimmy, and you know this goes for you, too, that they've turned over a new page in the history of our country. And I'll be counting on them to turn a lot more as we go along."

V.

Morning flowed down out of Princeton about the same time it brightened the sky above Washington, DC. George was up at the usual time, having decided to get a good night's sleep. But by the time he sat down for a continental breakfast, a haggard Wolf Blitzer was ready to announce the final results.

"Ladies and gentlemen, some of you may just be waking up and others may have been with us throughout this long and exciting night.

"For those of you who have just joined us, we have followed the erratic development, the ups and downs of this most curious election. Beginning yesterday evening at about eight thirty, we received reports that polling stations throughout the country showed record turnouts. Although the count is not yet complete, it seems certain that this presidential election has attracted more than 87 percent of registered voters. A huge *first*.

"That is sensational enough in itself. But the second fact is even more amazing. George Franklin, an unknown college professor as late as last April, has been running neck and neck with Charles Plympton, while James Singleton, the Republican candidate, has definitely been eliminated from the race. With only 46 percent of the votes counted and only a few states' returns reported, we have witnessed a massive vote for Professor Franklin. This has increased during the past two hours. Due to the slowness with which individual ballots can be counted, it may be another day before the tally is complete. However—"

An excited look came over Wolf's normally calm face as he received a message over his ear phone; he touched his index finger to his ear and nodded.

"Ladies and gentlemen, the computer has finally been able to talk, and we feel confident that we can now predict the winner."

A hush fell in the television studio. All the fidgeting and noise making of the production crew went silent. Everyone's attention was riveted on the triangular desk. Forks and spoons all over America stopped in midair as the famous reporter continued.

"Franklin has won!"

All the tension, controlled for days, flowed out of millions of throats.

VI.

When it was finally safe to announce the winner, most of the country's newspapers didn't exactly know how to go about it. Right up to the last minute, George Franklin carried his challenge forward into the White House. And in fact, many of the early editions more or less flipped a coin and decided to announce his victory in spite of the shades of Harry S. Truman. The machine had almost been defeated by the man.

As for the group gathered at Catherine's mansion, weary eyed, to say the least, the final announcement came as an anticlimax. It would be ridiculous to say that they didn't care about the results, but they were obviously tied to an ideal that went beyond the counting of votes. When they learned that George would be the next president of the United States, they broke out another bottle of champagne and toasted democracy, just as enthusiastically as you might imagine.

Catherine smiled at Brad and said, "Looks like you'll have to go back to being a freshman!"

They all knew a turning point had been reached in American politics, one that would mark the future history of the country. They would pass through the gates of responsibility and discover a completely new set of rules. The coercion of money and power would slowly disintegrate before the imperative of a new and more compassionate majority. The people, the usually silent and docile millions, would no longer stand for the kind of pollution created by selfish, hypocritical, and narrow-minded public servants.

This great nation was going to stop decaying.

The symbolic depth of this truth was perhaps best stated by the impressive headlines of Billy Flinders' paper in Washington. They were formulated over a cup of coffee at Barney's Café and accepted by the editor-in-chief over the phone: "Franklin, the people's president."

George, steadfastly serene in his small house on Hillside Road, was finally reached by the mob of reporters, anxious to hear his reaction. They focused their cameras on the front door as he opened it and walked out on the front porch. Well dressed and clear eyed, his demeanor was just as serious as it had been during the campaign. Before addressing the nation, he traced an imaginary signature in the air and motioned the excited news crews to be silent.

"The people of the United States, in large numbers, have just accomplished the important act of proclaiming a new government, duly elected through the *democratic* process. In performing this civic duty by writing in their candidate's name, they have proven beyond a shadow of a doubt how strong each American voter is and how ready they are to assume the awesome responsibilities of their nation. This is something that I applaud from the bottom of my heart. Another American, much more eloquent than I, stated the truth at the center of this campaign over a century ago. And without sounding too much like a college professor, I want to finish my statement by quoting him:

> 'There will never be a really free and enlightened State until the State comes to recognize the individual as a higher and independent power, from which all its own power and authority are derived, and treats him accordingly.'

That other American was Henry David Thoreau."

The End